DRAGON EVER AFTER

A Here Be Dragons Novel

LOUISA MASTERS

Note to self: You can't teach an old dragon new tricks… he likes to invent his own.

After half a century of chaos, my retirement from leading the Community of Species Government has been bliss. No more hellhounds playing pranks. No more snippy demons demanding my attention. No more cajoling money from the wealthy to support the community. Just peace while I avoid my overbearing father and try to work out what my next steps will be.

Although… maybe three years of peace is enough. It might even be starting to get… boring. In fact, an adolescent dragon crash-landing on my landlord's shed is just the kind of excitement I need—especially when he brings his species leader to my door.

Brandt. Wing leader of all dragons, suave, sexy, and… slightly unhinged. It doesn't take much for him to convince me to give up my solitude and spend some time getting to know him. It's hard to care about the future when I've got a dragon of my own to "play" with. Naked dragon rides for the win, right?

But Brandt's the leader of his people, on call for them all the time, and I've left that part of my life behind me. Plus my father insists I should fulfil my duty to the family by getting a nine-to-five job and "marrying well." That's not what I want, but riding herd on a group of beings who fly, breathe fire, and could literally crush me beneath their feet would be a huge challenge, especially since Brandt's kind of loose with rules.

It all comes down to how much I want my very own dragon ever after.

CHAPTER ONE

Percy

I LIFT my head from the mediocre book I'm reading and frown. What's that whistling sound? It's almost like something's—

CRASH!!!

—falling from the sky at a high velocity.

That something seems to have landed on—or rather, *through*—the roof of the shed at the back of my rented house. I cock my head and listen for a moment, just in case it's a bomb that's about to explode because enemy secret agents have misidentified me as their target. Yes, I've been reading too many books and watching too many movies lately. I'm trying to catch up on all the things I haven't had time for in so long, but unfortunately, they seem to be slowly affecting my judgment. Like yesterday, when the shadow of the tree beside the back door fell across the doorway and my brain refused to allow me to walk through it because it might be Satan's doorway to hell. Never mind that I, of all people, *definitely* know that neither Satan nor hell exist. Lucifer is a government title, not a religious entity.

This is what too much time in imaginary worlds does to you.

Fortunately, from the sound of what seems to be rather creative swearing in a language I'm just starting to learn, it's not a bomb.

Of course, some would argue that a bomb is less destructive and far less trouble than a young dragon, so…

I put my Kindle down, somewhat relieved to not yet have to make the decision whether to finish this book or abandon it, and head for the back door. The tenor of the voice indicates youth, but even young dragons are large, so I'm not sure how much of the shed will be left. How to explain that to my human landlord?

Though it's dark outside in a way that city people could never understand without experiencing it, I don't have any trouble seeing that the shed is, in fact… flattened. Trying to remember if there was anything valuable—or flammable—inside, I stroll across the stretch of grass that separates it from the house and bite back a smile. The young dragon, who's shifted back to biped form and is wearing what looks like pajamas, swears like a trooper and attempts to clamber free from the wreckage.

Stopping a few feet away, I clear my throat.

The curses cut off midword, and he whips around, a very dragonish snarl coming from his throat. I hold my hands up, palms out, in the universal—interdimensional, actually—sign that I mean no harm.

"Are you unhurt?" I ask, then attempt to repeat it in elvish. My pronunciation is lacking, and I'm pretty sure I got the syntax wrong, but he instantly relaxes, presumably as he realizes I'm not human and thus he doesn't have to hide his species.

"I'm fine, thank you, sir," he says politely—in English. I guess my elvish is even worse than I thought. "I'm very, very sorry about your building. My family will repair it. Um…" He looks down at the rubble surrounding him. "Replace it."

"Don't worry about it," I assure him. "As long as you're not hurt. Would you like some help getting free?"

Sighing gustily with exasperation in the way that only teenagers can, he glares at the mess and says, "If it's not too much trouble."

Luckily, he's not actually stuck. If he'd stayed in his dragon form, it would have been simple for him to step over the mess, but some of the chunks of tin roof and other bits of the structure are a bit large for him to easily climb over in biped form. I help him clear a path out, and ten minutes later he's standing on the grass and blowing out a breath of relief.

That quickly changes. "My parents are not going to be happy about this," he says glumly, observing the wreckage from the outside.

"Maybe not," I concede, "but they'll be thrilled you're safe. Are you sure you're not injured?" He's probably sick of me asking, but if there's one thing I know about adolescents, it's that they often play down injuries —unless they need to get out of school or chores. Plus, the adrenaline rush of having crashed might have masked the signs of injury before, but it should be settling now. I skim my gaze over him again. He's dropped the glamor that would make him appear human, the differences most apparent in his sharply pointed ears and the prominent bone structure of his forehead and around his eyes, which gleam with that otherness that indicates dragon, not elf.

He shakes his head. "Just some scratches and bruises. I wasn't really *falling*, you know? Well, I was, but it was mostly a controlled fall. I just misjudged when to pull out of it."

Not for the first time, I marvel over how easily the young dragons and elves have picked up teenage syntax and slang habits. It's been only three years since they migrated to Earth when their own dimension collapsed, but this kid sounds like he's been speaking English his whole life.

"Practicing dive bombs?" I guess, and a guilty expression flashes across his face.

"Not *exactly*," he hedges, and I stifle a grin.

"Well, you'll have some time to think about what *exactly* you were doing while we wait for your parents to come and collect you. Do you have a phone with you? You can use mine if you don't." It's not likely that he doesn't. The one thing that elves and dragons universally adore about Earth is cell phones.

He squints slightly, as though thinking. It certainly can't be because of the light—the moon's not out, and while the stars are an array of sparkling glory, they're not bright enough to cause him to squint.

"I could go home by myself," he suggests, then glances around. "I think. Where exactly am I?"

Uh-huh.

"Somewhere your parents can pick you up from," I say firmly. I don't use my firm voice very often, especially not anymore, but this seems like a good time for it. "Phone?"

Sighing again, he drags a smartphone from his

pocket and stares glumly at it. "As soon as I turn it on, they'll be able to track it and then they'll know I'm not where I'm supposed to be."

Faint misgivings stir inside me. "Is that bad?" I ask carefully, trying to get a sense of whether his parents mistreat him without saying anything that might make him defensive. I won't send him back to a place or people where he's unsafe. I have connections to high-ranking dragons. I can make sure he's protected.

"They'll ground me for *weeks*," he complains, and that little clutch of tension in my belly loosens. Just a teenage desire to avoid deserved consequences, then. "And they'll lecture me for *hours* about not sneaking out to fly unsupervised. I'm a *dragon*. I have a *natural flying instinct*. I don't need to be supervised."

I have to cough so I won't laugh in his face. He's just too adorable. It's still hard for me to tell dragon ages, because they age so differently from us, but in shifter equivalent years, he seems to be around thirteen. That plays out in the fact that his parents still don't want him flying alone. Dragons, unlike Earth shifters, are not born in biped form. I'm still not entirely sure exactly how their reproductive process works, but I do know that baby dragons hatch from eggs and can fly within the first few years of life—but they're clumsy. I had the honor of seeing a dragon toddler fly once, and it was the cutest damn thing ever.

"You still need to call them," I say solemnly, not mentioning that his "natural flying instinct" resulted in the annihilation of my landlord's shed.

He heaves another dramatic sigh, then turns on his phone.

It immediately rings, and he winces. "I guess they

realized I'm not in bed," he mutters, then swipes a finger across the screen and lifts it to his ear. "Hey, Dad."

My shifter hearing means I have no trouble eavesdropping on what his father says, though honestly, the volume with which he speaks would probably make it audible to even a human. My elvish is still a bit too rudimentary to catch every word at that speed, but he seems to be demanding to know where the kid is and if he's okay. Then there's something about coughing twice if he's in danger or has been stolen.

I think I like his dad.

"I'm fine, Dad," the kid—I really should have asked his name—says in English. He has manners, I'll say that for him. "I… uh… okay, so you're not allowed to be mad. Not just yet, anyway."

There's a brief silence on the other end of the line. "Who's there with you?" his dad demands, switching to English also.

"The, uh, the man whose shed I crashed into? But I'm okay! The shed isn't, but I am, and that's a good thing, right?"

"Give me strength," his father mutters. "You crashed into a shed? Are you sure you're not hurt?"

"Positive," the kid declares cheerfully, clearly happy to not be talking about the shed or the fact that he sneaked out and was flying without permission. "And this man—sorry, sir, what was your name?"

"Percy Caraway," I tell him. He might not recognize it, but his father likely will, and it might reassure him somewhat.

"Mr. Caraway asked me heaps of times if I was okay and then said I needed to call you, so I'm safe here until you can come and get me. Maybe tomorrow? It's late, and you should get some rest."

"I should—" His father cuts himself off, takes a breath so deep I can hear it clearly, and then counts to ten in a mutter. "Benisch, how can you possibly think I could *get some rest* knowing that you crashed into a shed and are now somewhere I don't even know where with a stranger? Do you even understand how worried we've been? You were gone from your bed in the middle of the night and your phone was off! We called the wing leader to arrange search parties!" He pauses. "Wait. Did you say Percy Caraway?"

The kid—Benisch—looks at me again. "Are you like a famous murderer or something?"

His dad makes a choking sound.

"No," I assure him, managing to keep a straight face. "Could I speak with your dad?"

Benisch hands over the phone without question and wanders back over to poke around in the wreckage of the shed. I guess it's lucky for him I'm *not* a "famous murderer" who lies about it when asked.

"Hello?" I say into the handset. "This is Percy Caraway."

"Vridel Nandag," he says automatically. "Excuse me, are you the Percy Caraway who used to be the lucifer?"

"I am," I confirm, but his name has already rung bells in my head. "I believe we might have met once." It was not long after the migration, when the dragons were still struggling to recover from everything that happened. At Wing Leader Brandt's request, some of us who were senior at the Community of Species Government—CSG—visited the dragon communities to answer questions. Vridel was our guide, due entirely to the fact that his translator spell was more attuned than any of the other dragons'. I remember him as being intelligent, thoughtful, and having a wicked sense of humor.

"We did," he says, relief heavy in his tone. "This is good. Forgive me, I'm very off-balance right now. We really thought…" He trails off and takes a deep breath. "Benisch is really unhurt?"

"He hasn't been checked by a medic, but he says he's fine and he's been walking around and talking with no signs of pain or injury," I reassure him.

Vridel takes another deep breath. "Good. Good. And he destroyed your shed?"

I turn to look at the remnants of what once was a sturdy structure. Benisch must be a good-sized dragon already, despite his youth. "Not mine, my landlord's, but I'm afraid so. As far as I understand, it was something to do with a controlled fall he misjudged."

"Controlled, huh?" Vridel says dryly, sounding a little more collected now that he knows his son is okay. "The day that fledgling learns what control actually is, I'm throwing a party the likes of which no world has ever seen."

I chuckle. "You're not the first parent who's said something like that to me," I commiserate.

"I'm sure I'm not. I'll come and collect him, and we can discuss how to replace the shed. Is your landlord part of the community or a human? We have developed strategies to explain property damage caused by fledglings to humans. Maybe we could say a light plane crashed into it." He pauses. "Did the noise wake your neighbors?"

"No need to worry about that," I assure him. "I'm

on acreage out here. The nearest neighbors are over half a kilometer away, and it's dark enough that they wouldn't have seen anything even if they heard something and looked out the window."

"Well, that's good luck, at least. Let me just track Benisch's phone and work out which direction…" His voice fades and then he swears in elvish. "Lucifer—I mean, Mr. Caraway—"

"Percy is fine," I tell him, unable to stop myself from wincing.

"—are you in Western Australia?"

The disbelief in his voice concerns me. Is he not as close as I thought? Dragons have mostly settled in rural areas, since it gives them greater scope to fly without being seen by humans. Western Australia—especially this northern part—is a great place for that, hence me not being surprised to find a young dragon in my backyard. But Vridel's shock makes me wonder where their home could actually be. The nearest other state to here isn't a state at all, but the Northern Territory, and it's about eight hundred kilometers—or five hundred miles —away. The next closest place that could sustain a dragon settlement is Indonesia, to the north, but that's even farther away—and with open ocean to cross, which surely even a reckless teen wouldn't try alone. Dragons fly fast—faster than most planes, almost as fast as the speed of sound—but that's a *lot* of air to cover in what can only have been a few hours.

"Yes," I say cautiously. "Not too far outside Broome. Why? Where are you?"

"Queensland," he says faintly. "Near Gympie."

It's only sheer will that keeps me from saying something vulgar. That's the breadth of the country. If any airline flew direct from Gympie to Broome, it would take—I do a quick calculation—around five hours.

I look back over at Benisch, who's still prodding the twisted corrugated iron that broke his fall, but also yawning. That kid has serious stamina to have gotten this far.

"I know there's a time difference," I say, trying to remember if they're two hours ahead or three. Two, I think, since Queensland also doesn't practice daylight saving. "But that still seems like he covered a lot of ground in a very short time." Last time I looked at the clock, it was just past eleven thirty. Benisch must have snuck out right after bedtime and flown pretty much straight here, and that seems unusual for a teenager. Wouldn't he have been more interested in trying out tricks and testing his aerial acrobatics than flying west in a straight line for hours?

"He must have learned how to skip," Vridel mutters. "That's the only explanation. I'll talk to him about it when I get there, see if I can work out exactly what happened. It's going to take me longer than I thought, and—"

There's a commotion on his end of the line, and he says, "Excuse me a moment, please, Luci—I mean, Percy."

"Of course."

There's a rustle as he puts his hand over the microphone, but I can still hear the murmur of voices and pick out the occasional word—the benefit of shifter hearing. Vridel seems to be explaining the situation to someone—his mate, perhaps?

Then I hear another voice, one I recognize, one I came to know pretty well in the months after the migration before I left CSG. A voice that has always, no matter what it was saying, sent shivers through me.

Wing Leader Brandt.

Aka the sexiest beast (no pun intended) to ever walk the earth. Fly the skies. Whatever. You know what I mean.

I don't know how I managed to keep my attraction to him to myself, but I did. Nobody suspected—thank goodness. Because as much as I love the people who worked for me at CSG, if they'd known, there would have been a conspiracy to get me and Brandt together. I know this because I was part of previous conspiracies to get some of them together with their significant others.

Now that I think of it, Vridel did tell Benisch earlier that they'd called the wing leader to arrange search parties. And even though I don't know Brandt intimately (sigh), it doesn't surprise me that he'd drop everything and cross the Pacific Ocean to come to the aid of a child in need. Although… that's a long flight in a short time. Something to do with that skipping thing Vridel mentioned?

I have so many questions.

They'll have to wait, though. Vridel and Brandt seem to be wrapping up their conversation, and the priority right now needs to be Benisch.

"Percy?" The voice in my ear is not Vridel's, and I shove down the butterflies that erupt inside me. How can any man have a voice capable of wreaking such havoc on my limbic system?

"Brandt," I squeak, then cringe and close my eyes. "Uh…" I clear my throat. "Sorry. I think I… swallowed a bug." What is happening to me? I don't get flustered like this—*ever*.

"A juicy one, I hope," he says blithely, then fortunately continues, since I have no idea how to answer that. "It's good to hear your voice. Especially since the circumstances are happy rather than tragic."

"Yes," I agree. "I'm so glad to have been able to set Vridel's mind at rest."

"We're all so relieved. We haven't had one of our young go missing since… well, you remember."

Indeed I do. I also remember her rescue. Vividly, and in great detail. After all, that was the day my life changed once more.

"I'm just glad none of you have to go through that again." My voice seems hoarse, and I clear my throat. "So… Vridel probably told you that young Benisch traveled farther than expected."

Brandt laughs. "These fledglings, always keeping us on our toes! We need to guard better against complacency. Vridel and I will come to fetch him, but if it's okay with you, I'd like to get a few hours' rest first. I've just had a long flight."

"Uh-huh," I say, diplomatically not demanding to know how he got to Australia so quickly. "That's fine. Benisch seems to be somewhat tired," I add, glancing over to where the boy is now lying in the scrubby grass with his eyes closed. Shit. "Benisch, why don't you go into the house and lie on the couch?" I call. I don't want to say "because of snakes" and scare him, but it's a valid concern.

I think. Are snakes likely to bother dragons? Are they even venomous to dragons?

Benisch makes a grumbling sound but doesn't move, and I'm just wondering if I'll need to insist and explain why it's a bad idea to lie on the ground in the Aussie outback with your eyes closed when he heaves himself up and shuffles toward the house.

"Sorry about that," I tell Brandt, keeping my gaze on the kid until the screen door has slammed behind him. "I figured he'd be more comfortable inside. Uh, if you want to get some rest and come out here tomorrow, I can get him settled in the spare room"—one of four—"for the night and then keep him out of trouble until you arrive."

"That would be wonderful. We know he'll be safe with you. Thank you so much, Percy."

"It's no trouble," I say, heading toward the house. "Is there anything I should know?"

"Well, he's likely exhausted after coming all that way, so you won't need to guard against any more midnight excursions," Brandt says dryly. "If you could make sure he drinks a few gallons of water before bed, that would be good."

"Sure, I— A few *gallons*?" Is he a boy or a fish?

"Yes, he needs to rehydrate. The young ones always forget how much energy flying takes. If he's hungry, could you give him something with a lot of protein? And then again in the morning."

I enter the house and close the door behind me. "Steak and eggs?" I suggest. Being a shifter myself— although cat, rather than dragon—I understand the hunger that comes after changing form. I should have realized earlier that Benisch would be hungry—and his exhaustion now might well be partly because he's dehydrated.

"Perfect," Brandt approves.

"Do his parents want to speak to him again?" I pad through the house to the living room and find the grubby, tired preteen sprawled on the couch. He pries an eyelid open as I approach.

"Yes, please," Brandt says. "I want a word with him first, though."

"Okay, hold on and I'll pass you over to him. See you tomorrow." I pull the phone away from my ear and ask Benisch, "Would you like something to eat?"

He nods slowly, as though he's too exhausted even to move his head, and both sympathy and amusement twine through me.

"I'm going to make you something," I promise. "Wing Leader Brandt and your parents want to talk to you, then you can eat and get some sleep, okay?"

He makes that grumbling sound again, then levers himself slowly into a sitting position and holds out his hand for the phone. "Thank you," he says, holding on to his manners even while imitating a sleepy bear. I pass him his phone, then make a strategic retreat to the kitchen.

Well, this night certainly took a turn.

I listen with half an ear to Benisch's side of the conversation—which seems to consist mostly of him fervently agreeing and promising he won't do things—as I prep his food. From what I remember, dragons have a fairly similar metabolism and eating habits to Earth shifters, so he's probably going to want his steaks rare, or medium at the most.

By the time he shuffles in, phone in hand, the eggs are ready and the steak nearly so. I've laid a place setting for him at the table, along with a big jug of water to start him off. He reaches for it immediately and drains it faster than I would have thought possible. Then he shoots me a guilty look.

"Sorry. I should have used a glass."

I smile at him, set his plate on the table, and take the pitcher to refill it. "Don't worry about that. Thirst sometimes overtakes manners. Why don't you get started on that while I make up a bed for you?" I set the newly full pitcher beside him and wait just long enough to see him digging into his food.

Hmm. Two rib-eyes and four eggs might not be enough.

That's okay. I have more.

I grab sheets from the linen closet, get halfway down the hall, then have to go back and check which shelf they were on. The owner, who rented the place to me fully furnished and stocked, has the shelves labeled. Each shelf is stocked with sheets or towels or whatever for a specific room. He asked me very seriously to be careful not to mix them up. Far be it from me to mess with his system, especially since he asked me no questions about why I wanted to live alone in almost the middle of nowhere for six months.

By the time I've made up the bed, checked under it and in the closet for snakes and spiders—since the room's been unused for months—switched on the fan, and returned to the kitchen, Benisch is scraping up the last of his food. From the looks of him, he'd lick the plate if he didn't know I was watching. The pitcher is empty again, and I take it to the sink to fill. Good thing this property has big water tanks.

"Would you like more food?" I ask, and he nods.

"Please. If it's okay. Maybe just a couple more eggs?" He smiles sheepishly. "I didn't realize how hungry I was." He looks a little better now than he did only fifteen minutes ago—there's more color in his face, and his gaze is sharper.

"Of course it's okay." I crack another two eggs into the pan, and he comes to stand beside me as they cook, taking the pitcher but this time sipping from it instead of gulping.

"Brandt said I've flown all the way across the country. Is that true? I've never done that before. My friends are never going to believe it—and they'll be so jealous."

Yep. Definitely feeling better.

"You did. I'm not sure how you managed it in that timeframe, but we're about two hours' drive from Broome here. Do you know where Broome is?"

He nods. "On the coast of Western Australia. They grow pearls there."

Grow pearls? Close enough. "Yes. So you've come a long way."

He falls quiet for a moment, then sighs. "I'm going to be in so much trouble when they're finished being glad I'm okay."

"Probably," I agree. "You scared them a lot. And even more now that they know how far you came and how many bad things could have happened along the way."

Nodding, he sips the water again. "Dad and Brandt said I had to tell you not to worry about humans seeing me. I kept up the distortion shield the whole way—I swear I did. And I didn't see any planes or anything anyway that would have been close enough to see me in the dark, even if I did let the spell go. But I didn't. I kept it up all the way, right up until I crashed and shifted back." His earnest explanation is accompanied by solid eye contact.

"Thank you," I tell him solemnly, a little amused but mostly relieved. Exposure to humans would be so, so bad. Especially now, with everyone in the community still adjusting to the changes from a few years back, when the elves and dragons migrated to Earth. "I appreciate that, and so does everyone else in the community."

"Brandt said you used to be the lucifer when we first moved here. Is that true?"

I scrape his eggs out of the pan and onto his plate. "Yes. That's how I met him and your dad."

"Thank you for letting us come here." There's a slight quaver to his voice. Not tears exactly, but maybe the precursor to them. "I don't remember before we had to live in the shield, but I think it would have been like living here—we could fly anytime without needing to worry about boundaries. And there wouldn't have been people disappearing all the time. I kind of miss home anyway, but I really like it here, and I'm *really* glad we're not all dead."

I turn away to put his plate on the table, needing a moment to hide my face. It still makes me feel sick to know how close the elves and dragons came to being wiped out. All because a greedy, selfish man refused to think of anyone other than himself. Éibhear's insistence on using temporal portals—essentially, time travel—resulted in the slow collapse of the dimension the dragons and elves lived in. Moments of existence from the past just ceased to exist, and people who'd been born in those moments would disappear from one second to the next. The planet they lived on became unstable, falling to pieces around them, and the survivors were forced to live within a shield bubble, waiting for the end to come.

"I'm really glad you're not all dead too," I say when I feel more in control. "And I'm sad for you that you lost your home, but we're all so happy to have you here."

He grins at me, then resumes his place at the table and digs into the eggs. I leave him to it and begin a circuit of the house, checking that lights are off and closing some of the doors and windows. It's not necessary, since there's about zero chance of anyone trying to break in out here and I'd hear and smell them before they got close, anyway, but some habits are hard to break. I also stop by my bedroom and grab a T-shirt and some cotton athletic shorts for Benisch to sleep in. They'll be a bit loose—although not that much. I'm not exactly a big man—but the drawstring should keep them on. I lay them on his bed.

Back in the kitchen, Benisch is stacking his plate and cutlery in the dishwasher.

"Does the frypan go in there too? The ones at my house do, but my friend Tonis says at his house, they have to wash them by hand," he tells me without turning around.

"It can go in." I note that the pitcher is once again empty and mentally calculate how much water he's drunk. "Do you want me to get a water bottle for you to take to bed, in case you want more during the night?"

He turns, his face alight with a smile. He seems a cheerful kid. "Could you? I'm going to have some more now, but I'm pretty sure I'll get thirsty later too."

I rummage through one of the cupboards as he refills the pitcher, eventually finding an insulated bottle. It won't hold quite as much water as the pitcher, but he can refill it if he needs to. I fill it up while he gulps down the contents of the pitcher, then hand it to him and lead the way out of the kitchen, flipping off the light as I go.

The house is really much too large for just me, but it's not like there are a whole lot of isolated properties in the area available for short-term rental. I would have found something more my size closer to Broome, or in the town itself, but that wouldn't have given me the privacy or acreage I wanted. Out here, with the nearest neighbor nowhere close, I can comfortably shift and let my cat lie out in the sun all afternoon, or prowl through the scrub, hunting lizards—purely catch-and-release, of course. My cat's something of a food snob and wouldn't eat lizard unless he was starving, especially when there's perfectly good steak in the fridge. I, on the other hand, have happily tried cuisine from all over the world, including lizards and snakes, and my expert opinion is that it's all in the seasoning. But regardless, both my cat and I like having this solitude after so many years of being at the beck and call of others. And it's not like I'm planning to be here for that long—my lease is up soon, and I'll move on to the next place. Somewhere in the Indonesian rainforests, maybe; give my cat a chance to play in some trees.

"This is your room," I tell Benisch, gesturing to the open doorway. The bedside lamp is on, casting a warm glow over the turned-down bed. "There's a bathroom just across the hall here. Give me a few minutes and I'll find you a spare toothbrush—and a washcloth." He did fly across the country, after all. He could probably do with a wash. "Or you can have a shower, if you want."

From the way his face screws up, I guess he's still at that doesn't-ever-want-to-wash age, not yet the spends-too-long-in-the-shower age.

"Just the washcloth, then," I compromise, because it's totally not my job to make him shower. His dad can deal with that tomorrow. "Do you need anything else tonight?"

He shakes his head. "No, thank you. I just want to sleep now." As if on cue, a huge yawn overtakes him, and I can't help but smile. Kids of any species are just so damn cute.

Mostly.

I leave him to change and go dig out a new toothbrush and clean washcloth. His eyes are already drooping when I bring them to him, and he shuffles into the bathroom like a zombie. I don't want him to think I'm hovering, but I'm kind of afraid he'll just fall asleep on his feet and topple over, cracking his head on the vanity, so I retreat to my bedroom but wait just inside the door, unseen but ready to spring forth if I hear anything that sounds like an injury in the making.

I needn't have worried, though, because a few minutes later the water goes off and I hear him shuffling back to his room. There's the creak of the mattress, a click as he turns off the lamp, and then silence.

I close my door most of the way and get ready for bed. It's not until I'm lying in the darkness, my brain sinking into sleep, that a thought strikes me, and I surge to full awareness.

Brandt's coming here tomorrow.

I'll need to see him. Talk to him. Not be an idiot in his presence. Definitely keep my hands to myself and not stroke them through his silky, silver-threaded dark hair.

Well, crap.

CHAPTER TWO

Brandt

I squint down at the ground far below me, looking for a landmark. We should be nearly there now, but in such a rural area with so few points to fix on, it's hard to know how much farther we need to go. Endless dusty, scrubby land begins to look the same after a while, even from the air, where we have better perspective. We've stopped a few times to recheck where Vridel's tracking app has pinpointed Benisch's phone to and to adjust course. The last twenty minutes, we've basically been following the main highway, since Percy's house is supposedly not far off it, and just hoping it leaps out at us.

Navigating while flying is somewhat of a precarious art.

My eye catches on something up ahead, and I laugh. In my dragon form, it comes out as a grumbly huff. I've always rather liked the sound, and for a while in my younger days, I tried to emulate it in my biped form too. That was an epic failure and frightened a lot of people here on Earth when I visited—which was what finally induced me to give it up.

"Over there," I tell Vridel. *"See that wreckage? I bet that's the shed your son landed on."* Our dragon forms don't have a spoken language—although there are some situations where the noises we make convey our feelings quite clearly. Instead, we speak mind-to-mind. For most dragons, the telepathic ability can only be used in dragon form, but some of us who've been around for a long time can also manage it in biped form. Not that I'm bragging or anything.

"He did a thorough job," Vridel says dryly. *"Perhaps he's got a future in demolition. That's nice stable work."*

I laugh again, and we bank in that direction. It's a beautiful day for flying, clear as far as the eye can see with some lovely warm updrafts. My understanding is that this region will enter its wet season soon, but for now, there's not a cloud in sight.

We land cautiously beyond the wreckage of the shed, keeping it and some distance between us and the house, just in case we got it wrong. Not that anyone would see us anyway, with the distortion shield in force, but we're quite bulky, and having a human accidentally walk into us would be bad. Not to mention these kinds of properties often have dogs, and while the spell shields us from sight, dogs rely on smell and hearing far more than humans do.

There was no need to worry, though, because not ten seconds after we land, the back door bangs open and Benisch charges out of the house, grinning from ear to ear. Vridel sighs with relief, and we both let the distortion shield dissolve.

Before I can shift to my biped form, a whiff of

familiar scent catches my attention, and I glance back at the house. Percy is coming out the back door.

He's so pretty, with his soft brown hair and warm brown eyes. I forgot how attractive he is. He's smaller than me, like most felid shifters, perhaps five foot seven and slimly built. And that lovely soothing air he has… he's like the living embodiment of an afternoon with a book, or a long massage. Just seeing him is enough to make me relax.

He, on the other hand, is not relaxed by the sight of us. Me? He's staring. At first his jaw dropped, but he seems to have gotten that under control now and is just fixed on me.

"Brandt?" a voice asks, and I swing my head around to see Vridel in biped form, arms around his son, both of them looking at me. "Do you plan to remain in dragon form?"

Crap. That's probably why Percy's staring—I don't think he's seen me in dragon form before. I sneak another glance at him, and yes, there's definite awe there. Well, I am rather a magnificent dragon, and I can't help preening just a little. I adjust my stance so the sun hits my scales, turning them from solid indigo to a slightly shimmery purple, and Percy's gasp is clearly audible even with the distance between us.

"Is Brandt okay?" Benisch asks Vridel, and I stop showing off and change into my biped form, taking a moment to straighten my clothes as I do.

"I'm fine, you troublemaker," I tell him, but far from being cowed—not that I'd want him to—he grins and throws his arms around my waist for a fierce hug.

"I didn't mean to cause trouble, but I'm glad to see you," he declares. I hug him back. We have so few fledglings left. We've never been especially populous, definitely not in comparison to other species, but what Éibhear did to our homeland devastated our numbers. Each and every remaining dragon is so precious to me now—especially the young ones.

"I'm glad to see you too. Although," I can't help adding, "people who don't mean to cause trouble usually stay in their beds at night." Not me. I've always loved to fly at night. As soon as I worked out how to flip the latch on my nursery window, I began slipping out. At one point, my parents had to take turns staying up to watch me—or fly with me. Young dragons are made for trouble.

But I'm not telling Benisch that.

He adopts a contrite, downcast expression, but ruins it by peeking up at me with mischief glinting in his eyes.

I swallow my laughter.

"Have you been a good guest?" I ask instead, and he nods.

"I helped clean the kitchen last night, and this morning I made my bed and helped Percy make breakfast."

"Mr. Caraway," his father corrects, but Benisch shrugs.

"He said to call him Percy because it helps him stay humble."

Like that man needs help staying humble. Even when he was the lucifer, he was the most self-effacing person I'd ever met.

Speaking of... my senses warn that he's approaching, and I turn and smile at him.

"Good morning," he says, stopping a few feet away. "Welcome."

Vridel steps forward, arm outstretched for the local custom of shaking hands. "Thank you so much," he says, clasping Percy's hand with both of his. "I owe you a debt beyond price."

Percy's gentle, soothing smile blooms across his face, and he replies, "There are no debts when it comes to the safety of children. I'm just glad I could help—and to see you again."

"Hey, I'm not a *child*," Benisch complains, and we all turn incredulous looks on him. He rolls his eyes and huffs. "Fine, whatever."

Vridel releases Percy's hand and steps back, and I surge forward, bypassing formality to grab him in a tight hug. After all, when you've stood shoulder-to-shoulder with a man in the fight to save existence, then watched him rip out the throat of the enemy, you earn the right to be more casual.

His arms come up to hug me back, which is good, because it gives me a little more time to feel the slender, toned length of his body against mine. I've wanted him since the day we met, but there were too many other things to focus on then—like impending doom—and then once the immediate danger had passed, there was so much to do in the aftermath, including helping my people to settle in this new dimension. Then Percy finished handing over the reins of CSG to Sam, the new lucifer, and… left.

"They're hugging for a really long time," Benisch observes. Percy stiffens against me, but not in the good way, so I reluctantly let him go.

"Friends hug when they haven't seen each other in a long time," Vridel informs his son, but then shoots me a sidelong glance with a quirked eyebrow that tells me he's not that naïve.

Percy clears his throat. "Won't you come in?" he asks politely. "I'm sure you're thirsty and probably hungry after such a long flight. Benisch and I prepared a snack to tide you over until lunch is ready."

"It's scones," Benisch informs us as he leads the way to the house. "And sausage rolls and some other stuff. We made the scones, but Percy says the sausage rolls were made from scratch too, even the pastry!"

"Do you like to cook?" I ask, fascinated, but Percy laughs.

"Not enough to make puff pastry from scratch," he says. "My neighbor in that direction"—he points north—"has a stall at the Broome market every Saturday. They sell gourmet foodstuffs, and if I'm standing by the gate with money in hand when they drive past, they'll stop and give me first pick of their products. Shirley makes the best sausage rolls I've ever tasted, and her jams are to die for. Jonno cures his own meat."

I can't stop the snort that bursts from me. Percy looks perplexed for a moment, then rolls his eyes. "Seriously? That's not even funny. It's kind of painful, if you think about it." He holds the door as we troop through, and I shrug.

"It's kind of funny. And maybe painful is what he likes."

"What are you talking about?" Benisch asks, and Vridel and Percy both glare at me.

"I'm making an unfunny and inappropriate joke," I tell him, and he groans.

"Why do grown-ups always do that? It's so weird.

Jokes should be *obviously* funny as soon as you hear them."

"Probably," I agree, just glad he's not asking me to explain it.

In the house, Percy shows us where we can wash up after our flight, and then Benisch comes to lead us to the kitchen. "Percy was going to set the table in the dining room, but I told him no, that's for company, and we're not company."

Vridel's lips twitch as he says solemnly, "Brandt is the wing leader of all dragons, Ben. Don't you think that deserves the dining room?"

Benisch looks me up and down. "Well… maybe. But if he wants to be treated like company, he needs to not tell inappropriate jokes. That's what family and friends do."

My heart melts and I grab him in a headlock. "Faaaaaaamillllyyyyyyyyy!" I yell, digging my knuckles gently into his scalp as he squeals with laughter and shrieks for me to let him go. By the time I do, he's breathless from laughter and Vridel and I are both grinning widely.

"So this is where you got to," a dry voice says. "Benisch, you were right. This unruly lot will be better in the kitchen."

I poke my tongue out at him and wriggle it. It's a perfectly innocent gesture, *I swear.* Just because Percy's smile slips away and he swallows, his eyes darkening, doesn't mean that's what I intended. It doesn't mean I want him to think about all the other things I could do with my long, flexible tongue.

Really.

Vridel coughs, shooting me a narrow-eyed look and

nodding to his son, so I guess my tongue-flirting wasn't as subtle as I'd thought. Which makes sense, because I'm not known for subtlety.

I meekly—well, with a semblance of meekness—draw my tongue back into my mouth and follow them into the kitchen, where there is food. Food that smells amazing. And big jugs of water on the table, too, reminding me how thirsty I am. Vridel and I made sure to drink every time we stopped to get our bearings, but it's still a long flight and very hot out there.

We settle, and Percy passes me and Vridel the water with a small smile. "Drink up."

"Thank you," Vridel says, grabbing one of the large tumblers and filling it like a gentleman. I cast a sideways look at Benisch, who's staring guiltily at the table, and then at Percy, who flicks a glance at the jug in my hand and then mimes lifting it to his mouth.

Ah. Well, far be it from me to show up one of my dragons.

I lift the jug and drink directly from it. Benisch's startled laughter rings out, and when I eventually lower the jug, he's grinning widely at me. Vridel, too. And Percy...

He's smiling, but there's a soft expression in his eyes that makes me feel thirty feet tall. In case you were wondering, that's almost twice the height of my dragon form... and almost the length.

"I'll get more water," Percy says, a thread of laughter in his voice, but I wave my hand in dissent and stand.

"I can get it," I tell him. The sink is right there, after all. Vridel fills all our glasses, then hands me his empty jug, and I refill them both and return to the table.

"Please, eat." Percy gestures to the array of food. None of us have to be asked twice.

There's the promised scones and sausage rolls—which are cousins to the American pigs in blankets—some sandwiches, what looks and smells like a peanut butter protein slice, and fruit. For the scones, there's a range of jams, creams, and curds.

Some species might call it a full meal, but it's the perfect midmorning snack for shifters.

I moan through a mouthful of scone with lemon curd, a piece of sausage roll in my hand ready to go into my mouth next.

"It's good, isn't it?" Percy says smugly. "Shirley has a gift." He sighs. "I'm going to miss her food when I move on."

"You're moving on?" Vridel asks politely between bites, and Percy nods.

"My lease is up in another five weeks, and the owner will be back."

"Are you going to find another house or go somewhere else?" Benisch asks. He's not eating quite as much as me and Vridel, but then, he is much smaller and has had two full meals already since his flight across the country.

Percy smiles indulgently at him, putting some more of the protein slice on his plate. "I'll go somewhere else. I like it here, but there are a lot of places I haven't seen yet. I'm enjoying getting to know all different parts of the world."

"Have you seen Gympie? It's nice there. You could live with us for a while."

A half-chewed bit of pastry lodges in my throat—

possibly because it just closed over with emotion. I love my young dragons.

Percy's smile is bright and wide. "Thank you, that's a very sweet offer. I have seen Gympie. I wouldn't mind coming back for a visit, but I think the next place I live might be a rainforest."

"There are rainforests in Queensland," Benisch persists. "They're not very close to us, but they're closer than here. It would be easy for us to visit if you were there."

"Benisch," Vridel starts, but Percy's still smiling.

"You mean the Daintree? It's lovely there, but I was thinking of a rainforest in a country I haven't spent much time in yet. Maybe Indonesia."

Benisch squints, and I get the distinct feeling he's trying to remember if he knows anything about Indonesia. Or maybe he's trying to calculate if it's too far to fly to.

"That's too far for you to fly," I say just as Vridel says, "You can't fly there by yourself."

Benisch rolls his eyes. "I'm not a baby," he mutters. "I came here by myself, didn't I? I even *skipped*."

Vridel puts down his strawberry. "Did you really want to remind me of that right now?"

"Aren't these scones *the best*?" Benisch asks, eyes wide, and Percy laughs again.

I really enjoy that sound. He never laughed when I knew him before—well, not often, anyway. The times didn't allow for much laughter, what with supervillains trying to take over this world after destroying ours.

"Please don't feel you need to answer," he begins, "but what's 'skipping'? I assume you're not talking about what children do."

I make my expression very stern and solemn. "You must never let anyone know you heard that term," I intone. "Never. Your safety depends on it."

For a moment, he's startled, shock taking over his face, but then he laughs so hard, I think he might actually hurt himself. Benisch and Vridel join him.

"You nearly had me," he chokes out. "For a second, I almost believed you."

Grinning, I snag some grapes. These cultivated grapes are very different from the wild ones I used to eat the last time I visited Earth, but I still like them a lot. I especially enjoy the many different varietals available now. And wine! What a wonderful idea that was. Humans really do have some good thoughts sometimes. "What gave me away?" I ask, plucking a delicious purple orb from the stem.

"I've spent the last fiftyish years surrounded by hellhounds," he says wryly. "Let's just say my bullshit meter is tuned very finely."

He has a point. Hellhound shifters are wacky—the kind of wacky that would change their species name to screw with their enemies and then keep it for nine thousand years. I give him a wide-eyed, pleading stare. "If anyone asks, could you tell them you believed me and were immediately fearful for your health?"

"If anyone… Why would anyone ask?" He sounds exasperated, but there's still a smile on his face. "And stop with those puppy eyes. You won't get me that way."

Puppy— I straighten indignantly, a grape dropping from my fingers. "Excuse me, I am a *dragon*, not a puppy. A puppy!" I exclaim in disgust. Don't get me wrong, I've met many puppies in recent years, and they are uniformly adorable and sweet. Fun fact, don't call hellhound children puppies. For some reason, the adults don't like it, and the whining lasts for-ev-er. Calling them pups is okay, though.

Hellhounds are ridiculous. Not like dragons. We're mighty, fearsome beasts known for our wisdom and sagaciousness.

I puff out my chest.

"I beg your pardon," Percy says sincerely, though that amused smile is still hovering around his lips. Has he truly stopped smiling at all since we arrived? I like this side of him. "I must be misremembering that time I visited a dragon settlement and saw a dozen adult dragons playing fetch."

Well… fuck.

"It wasn't *fetch*," I declare, although it really was. I know, because I was one of the dragons playing. I might be all mature and wise now, but occasionally I like to let loose with the younger crowd. It makes them more comfortable to come to me with their problems.

And playing fetch is fun.

"We're dragons, we *fly*. Fetch is a game played on the ground," I explain, and Vridel groans.

"O mighty wing leader of all dragons, shut up now," he mutters.

I subside huffily, and Percy reaches over to pat my hand. "There, there. I still think you're a mighty leader. Have some more grapes."

Involuntarily, I straighten, puffing my chest out again. Just a little.

Benisch is frowning, looking from me to Percy and back. "Dad? What are they doing?"

"Flirting," Vridel says sagely, and I drop my grape *again*.

Percy begins to splutter. "We aren't flirting… exactly."

Benisch watches him expectantly, waiting for an explanation, but it's Vridel who says, "What exactly would you say it was?"

Percy's face goes pink, and I kick Vridel under the table but miss and hit the table leg instead. The whole thing moves six inches, and one of the water glasses tips over. Good thing it's empty; water spilling everywhere would have been a distraction, and I'd really like to know why Percy thinks we're not flirting. I mean… I certainly was.

"Oh look," I say when everyone looks at me. "Percy has a rare Australian jumping table. What were you saying, Percy? Something about us flirting with each other, which would of course lead to getting to know each other better and all sorts of other wonderful things?"

He blinks. "Oh. *Oh.* Well… I suppose we were flirting, after all."

Yesssssss.

"Yeah, okay," Benisch says. "What exactly is flirting? I know it's kissing stuff, but what exactly is it?"

"That's a question for your dad to answer," I tell him happily and turn back to Percy. "So… you're planning to leave here soon? Could I tempt you to come back to the States with me? Just for a visit," I add hastily, not wanting to sound like an obsessed stalker desperate to move in with him. "I'm sure your friends would love to see you, and we could spend some time together."

That delightful pink color floods his cheeks again, and I marvel at the translucent delicacy of his skin. He has almost no facial hair—barely a trace of beard stubble. Just smooth, smooth skin. I like it.

"That… that sounds nice. Are you going back soon, though? I'd need to— Wait. Didn't you fly here last night?"

I nod and cast a stern look at Benisch, who's too busy listening to his father stutter through an explanation of dating rituals to notice. "Yes. It would have been a lovely flight, too, if not for the clawing panic of having a fledgling go missing."

He holds up a finger. "Hold that thought, because I want to come back to the whole flight time thing—don't think I've forgotten that you distracted me before. But what I mean is, if you flew yourself here, how could I go back *with you*? Or was that just a figure of speech?" He bites his lip, and there's a sparkle in his eyes—nerves? Excitement?

Could it be that the calm, quiet ex-lucifer wants to soar?

I stop myself from rubbing my hands together gleefully. Noah, delightful asshole that he is, told me it's weird and I look creepy doing it. I really don't know how Percy tolerated all the attitude in the people that surrounded him when he was lucifer.

"It can be anything you want it to be," I say, wiggling my brows, and he snorts.

"I don't know how much you know about felid shifters, but we can't fly," he points out. "Not without an airplane." A slight shudder accompanies the word, and I feel his revulsion. In the interest of trying everything Earth has to offer, I took a flight in one of the humans' airplanes.

Never. Again.

That's not flying. Flying is the joy of air currents and stretched wings and the glorious sight of the world below you and around you. What humans do… ugh. It's cramped and smelly and noisy. No thank you.

Which is what makes it such a pleasure to be able to tell Percy, "Ah, but you can." I wink. "It's nice to have a dragon at your… service."

"Brandt!" Vridel snaps. "My son is *right here*."

Oops. I'd forgotten about them. "We're talking about flying," I explain, pretending my last comment wasn't a double entendre at all. Nope. I was being totally innocent. "I was telling Percy that if he wants to come back to the States with me, I can fly him."

"You can?" Percy breathes, eyes wide. "H-How would that work? It's a long way. And… I'd really hate to die because I fell into the Pacific Ocean at a speed that made the water react like a solid surface."

"Can water do that?" Benisch asks in fascination. "I thought it only did that when it was ice."

Vridel sighs. "You'll probably learn about it at school. If you pay attention."

Benisch sighs too, looking so much like his father that I grin before turning back to Percy.

"I would never drop you," I say firmly. "But we'd use a harness anyway, just in case." I look at Vridel. "Do you have a harness?"

He shakes his head. "My old one fell apart a few centuries back, and I haven't needed one since. Someone will, though. I can ask around."

"Let's save that for another time," Percy interjects in a very diplomatic tone. "Brandt, I imagine you'll need to go back quite soon, and I have some things to organize here. I'll think about a visit and let you know."

I frown. That sounds like his yes has become a no.

Before I can push, he continues, "Now. Skipping. I'm guessing that's what allowed you to get to Australia so fast? And for Benisch to cross the country in just a few hours?"

I want to go back to the topic of him visiting—because if he's not going to, then I can try to rearrange my commitments to spend some time with my dragons here in Australia. Except… he's not staying in Australia. Do I have dragons in Indonesia? There isn't a full settlement, but surely someone is there who needs me to check in on them.

It's the silence that cues me in, and I look up to find three gazes fixed on me. "Did I miss something?"

"We're waiting for you to explain skipping to Percy," Vridel says with heavy-handed patience, as though he couldn't have explained it himself and left me to my very important thoughts. How can I seduce Percy if we're on different continents?

"Skipping is a dragon ability to use magic to compress distance," I explain. "It's kind of but not at all like the portals the elves use."

"Kind of but not at all like," Percy repeats. "Uh-huh. So in what ways are they alike?"

Maybe phone sex? One of my dragons discovered that some time back and was very enthusiastic, but like I told him, if I wanted someone to watch me stroke my own cock, I'd make one of those sexy videos and put it on the internet.

Interestingly, not one full day after I said that, Sam, the current lucifer, sent out a very frantic and detailed message about why putting sexy videos on the internet was something to be considered very seriously first.

"Very" was bolded, italicized, and underlined. I didn't read it all, since I have no more interest in putting sexy videos online than I do in having someone watch me pleasure myself. I'd much rather have someone else's hands on me… and mine on them.

"Brandt?" Percy's voice breaks into my daydream of running my hands all over his naked skin. Is it as smooth on the rest of his body as it is on his face? Or is he delightfully furry once the clothes come off? "What are the similarities between portals and skipping?"

I leer at him, unable to completely clear my mind of naked Percy. "Come fly with me, and I'll show you *everything*."

Vridel snickers, then says, "What Brandt meant to say, Ben, is that if Percy went flying with him, he'd be able to show him firsthand what skipping is like."

Benisch looks at him like he's lost his mind. "I know, Dad. I heard him. He just said that."

I guess I should be glad the innuendo was lost on him. And I definitely need to stop making innuendoes in front of the fledgling.

Stealing a glance at Percy, whose mouth is in a tight line—uh-oh—I push aside all thoughts of naked sexy times and pout remorsefully.

"There are only two similarities between portals and skipping," I say seriously, not wanting Percy to be mad at me. "They both allow the user to travel over distance within a shorter timeframe, and they both require use of the void."

The pinched expression on his pretty face fades. "The void… that's the space between existence, isn't it? Just emptiness?"

I nod. "Yes. Unlike the elves with their portals, we

don't create entrances and exits stacked neatly together and travel through the void. Instead, we…" I hesitate. It's rather esoteric, and I'm not sure how Percy will react. "We introduce void energy into the space we wish to travel through, reducing it to no-space and allowing us to skip over it to the next solid area."

His jaw drops.

"That's why we can't travel directly, the way the elves do with portals," I continue. "We can only skip over what we can see. Dragons have excellent eyesight, but even we can only see clearly for about twenty or so miles."

Percy closes his mouth, opens it, then closes it again. He picks up his glass, drains it, sets it down, and then asks, "When you say 'solid area,' do you mean that you're actually desolidifying a part of this world? Are you literally bringing the void, an expanse of empty nothingness, into this dimension, on this planet?"

He's getting a little pitchy toward the end, so I take a moment to think about the best way to answer.

"Yes and no. Mostly yes, but also no."

He nods. "Could you clarify, please? No, wait." He holds up a hand. "Does anyone at CSG know about this? Sam? Or David? Or even Alistair?"

"Of course. David found out first and asked lots of questions. Lots. And lots. He had a notebook with pages of questions, and he just kept adding more as I explained it. He's a bit uptight, isn't he? In the end, I told him to go home and have Caolan give him a good… er… seeing to." I was going to say "dicking," but Benisch would probably ask what that meant. It's a shame, because that phrase rolls beautifully off the tongue. Sexual slang has changed a lot since my last visit here, and I'm really enjoying learning all the new phrases. Plus, "a good dicking" just has a nice cadence.

Percy visibly relaxes. "So David knows all about it?"

"Yep!" I smile at him.

"And he's not worried?"

"Well, he was at first. But after I answered his questions, he seemed okay. He hasn't said anything about it since then, and that was…" I stop and think. "…maybe nine seasons ago?" I'm still getting used to the Earth custom of telling time. Some of their watches are very attractive—I have nineteen now, some shiny, some sparkly, some sober and sleek, a few with pictures of television characters—but this habit of breaking time into tiny increments is stupid. I should know, I've lived longer than any of them.

"That's fine, then. I trust David."

I clap a hand over my chest. "You don't trust me?" How could he not trust me? Didn't I stand at his side while we confronted the greatest danger to all of existence? We're brothers! Except not, because I'm not into that. No kink shaming—whatever cranks your motor—but I never liked my brother when he was alive, and the thought of fucking him makes my dick want to fall off.

Wait… how did I get onto that?

Percy. Right. Not brothers. He doesn't trust me.

"…not that I don't trust you," he's saying calmly. "Just that this is normal for you, but I don't understand it. If David has already asked all his questions and was happy with the outcome, then I don't need you to answer them again for me."

I sniffle.

He eyes me suspiciously. "Have you always been like

this, or have you spent too much time with hellhounds since you moved here?"

I think about it. "Both?"

A grin breaks over his face. "At least you're honest."

"Dad?" Benisch asks, and I love all my dragons, especially the fledglings, but right now, I could strangle him. "Are they doing it again?"

Vridel eyes me. "No. I'm not sure what they're doing now."

"Anyway," I interrupt, "so that's how skipping works. All dragons have the ability, but it doesn't manifest at the same time for all. Benisch has clearly developed early. It's instinctive, but failure to properly condition and train once the ability presents itself can result in *very bad things* happening." I cast a dark glance at Benisch, and he gulps.

"I didn't even know I was doing it," he protests. "I promise, I'll do whatever training you say I need to."

"We'll start on the way home," Vridel tells him. "Did you sleep properly last night?"

He nods.

"Really?"

"Really! I swear!"

"I checked in on him a few times, and he was out like a light," Percy interjects. "But if you'd rather he had more time to rest, you're welcome to stay for a few days."

"Yes!" I exclaim. "We'd love to."

"No," Vridel says exasperatedly, shaking his head at me. "My mate's waiting, and Brandt has duties to attend to. The extra rest isn't necessary anyway. He got a full night's sleep, and obviously plenty of food and water."

I glare at him. Why is he cockblocking me? Does he

have no understanding of what it's like to be single and horny?

"I need some extra rest," I proclaim. "I flew all the way from the States last night and then across Australia this morning. I've got *great* stamina, but I'm not a super-hero." I manage to resist the urge to leer at Percy when I mention my stamina, but I sneak a glance at him. That sweet, amused smile is back.

"I'll make sure you get a good lunch before you go," he assures me. "Would you like to go have a nap? I understand people of your advanced age like to do that in the middle of the day."

Is he…?

He is. He's teasing me!

As Benisch laughs and Vridel smirks, I decide that even if Percy doesn't want to come back to the US right now, it won't stop my campaign. Operation: Get Percy Naked is underway.

CHAPTER THREE

Percy

I STAND beside the remnants of the shed (which Vridel has already arranged to replace. The owner just needs to send him a list of items that were destroyed) and feel the backwash of air swamp me as the three dragons take flight. I can't see them, of course—they all activated the distortion shield before they took wing—but the image of them is burned into my brain.

Well… the image of *him*. Brandt. Benisch is an adorable fledgling, and Vridel just as impressive as all dragons are, but Brandt… wow.

Just wow.

I suppose a dragon doesn't get to be thirty thousand years old without becoming an incredible specimen of its species. Really incredible. With glorious deep blue scales that catch the light just right to reflect a hint of purple, and a body that's somehow both bulky and sleek…

The last of the dragon-induced breeze dies away, and I shake myself back to reality. Enough daydreaming.

I get out of the hot sun and go back into the house to find my phone, mentally calculating the time difference. A little after midnight, I think. I should probably wait until later tonight and call before David goes to work.

Settling into the comfy armchair by the front window, I hit speed dial two on my phone. I haven't used number one for nearly four years, but I still can't bring myself to change it.

The phone rings three times before David's sleepy voice says, "Are you okay?"

"Why do you always ask me that?" I demand, exasperated. I'm not a child—I was the leader of our people for decades, and before that, I managed to look after myself perfectly well for centuries. But David worries like a mother hen.

"Habit," he replies. "Also, it's the middle of the night."

"Not here, it isn't."

"So you called just to wake me up? No, go back to sleep—it's just Percy." That last bit is directed at Caolan, his sexy elf boyfriend who I can hear mumbling in the background.

"Percy? I like Percy." The words are much clearer, and there's a rustle of sheets.

"Caolan, what— Give me that!"

"Hi, Percy!" Caolan says into the phone, and now it's David's turn to mutter in the background. "How's the outback?"

"Hot," I tell him. "And I found a snake in the shower last week."

"What kind of snake?"

I pull the phone away from my ear and look at it. Is

he serious? Putting it back, I ask, "Does it matter? It was a snake. In my shower. Where it didn't belong. And I have no idea how it got there."

"What did you do? It's not still there, is it? Do you need me to come and carry it out with a spell?"

Fuck me, I wish I'd thought of that last week. Caolan could have been here via portal within literally seconds, and some quick elven spellcasting would have had that snake out of the house before the kettle boiled for tea. It would have been a much better solution than what I did, which was shift into my cat and snarl at it until I realized I was blocking the door, so even if it was inclined to leave, it couldn't. So I shifted back, googled what kind of snake it was—hard to say, since the species all seem to have so many variations—decided it was some kind of brown snake, and called my neighbor, who kindly came over with his shovel and took care of it for me.

I've been using the shower in the hall bathroom since.

"No, it's gone," I tell Caolan, leaving out the details. He'd get a kick out of the story, but he and David and the others would also worry. "My neighbor killed it for me."

He makes a sound that can only be described as a snort-laugh. "I watched you rip out the throat of your enemy, but you needed your neighbor to kill a snake?"

"It did kind of look like Tish," I joke, and he must have put it on speaker, because I hear David's laugh join his. I'm so glad we're at the point where we can laugh about what very nearly was a world-changing catastrophe.

"Aside from the snake, what have you been up to?" David asks. "Are you enjoying the area?"

"It's lovely here," I tell them. "Very different from what I'm used to, though. I'm not sure I could live here forever—especially not with the snakes—but for a change of pace, I'm liking it a lot. I've actually just had some visitors."

"Aside from the snake, you mean?" Caolan asks. "Was it a kangaroo? I'd really like to see a kangaroo. Next time we take a vacation, we're going to Australia so I can see kangaroos."

"I've told you, you can't make pets of them," David begins exasperatedly.

"It wasn't a kangaroo," I break in, because I've heard this argument before. Caolan always pretends to give in, but then David finds out he's been googling what kangaroos eat or whether they need a nest to sleep in. "It was Brandt, actually."

That throws them off. "Brandt?" Caolan says finally. "Our Brandt?"

"The wing leader of all the dragons who make my life a misery?" David adds, and I laugh.

"What have they done now?"

"What haven't they done? Did you hear about the glitter bomb at the Olympics?"

I wince. "The one in the natatorium?" Glitter had showered from the ceiling, covering thousands of spectators and the Olympic-sized pool right before the swim races began. It had been a disaster, with the races postponed and the entire schedule thrown off because the pool had to be cleaned.

"That was dragons," David says, and he's trying to sound pissed off, but there's a tiny thread of laughter in his voice. "I know I bitch a lot about hellhounds and the chaos they cause, but at least they don't have the ability to make themselves invisible."

"What do the humans think happened?" I ask, somewhat anxiously. It comes from a lifetime of knowing that the worst thing that could ever happen is for humans to discover we exist—and I say this even with the knowledge that the elves and dragons' entire dimension was destroyed.

"Sam and I smoothed it over," he says. "We simultaneously made it an error in the planning system and a miscommunication. In the end, they got so much publicity mileage out of it that I don't think they cared that much." He pauses. "So Brandt was there? Wait, Brandt was *there*? He was here yesterday. And he's supposed to be here again tomorrow!"

Before he can get too upset that his schedule will be disrupted, I interrupt, "He'll be there tomorrow. He came because he thought there was a missing fledgling."

"What?" they say simultaneously.

"It's fine; there wasn't. No, there was, but he just snuck out and went for a night flight alone, then ended up crashing into my shed." I tell them the whole story, finishing with the dragons' departure not long before. "Brandt was trying to explain this whole concept of skipping to me, but he just succeeded in terrifying me. Is it safe for them to be bringing the void into our dimension?"

"It's not exactly like that," Caolan begins, but David snorts.

"Stop. Your explanation is just as bad as Brandt's is. It's fine, Percy. I can send you the file with my notes, if you want, but I ran the math and it's safe."

"That's good enough for me." David is meticulous with that kind of detail. If he says it's safe, it is.

"So you had a fledgling drop in on you," Caolan says, with heavy emphasis on "drop in." "Get it? Did you get it?"

"We got it," David says dryly. "I thought I told you Alistair was wrong about puns being universally funny?"

I laugh.

"Well, I thought it was funny," Caolan defends.

"I did have a fledgling drop in," I say hastily, before they get sidetracked. They're adorable together, but most of their arguments end in kissing and groping, and I don't want to be stuck on the other end of the line while they do that. "He was very sweet. And it was wonderful to see Brandt again." I wince. "Wonderful" might have been overkill.

"Wonderful?" Of course Caolan pounces on it. I swear, as much as the elves are supposed to be the serious ones, he's just as bad as any dragon sometimes. "Seeing Brandt was wonderful? How wonderful?"

David sighs, but then rather than taking my side and telling Caolan to back off as I'm expecting, he says, "Did you and Brandt hook up?"

I sputter.

"Crap, you did!"

"No!" I exclaim. "Of course we didn't." The circumstances weren't right. I'm not saying that, though.

David waits. Even Caolan is quiet.

"We flirted a little," I finally admit. "He asked if I'd come back and spend some time getting to know him better."

"Caolan, put that phone down!" David snaps.

"But—"

"No! You can't text Alistair about this."

Oh dear. Oh *dear*. That would be bad. Very bad. I hold my breath and wait to see if David wins this battle.

"What about—"

"Not Andrew, either."

"But—"

"No!"

"Not even—"

"Caolan! This is Percy's business."

Caolan snickers. "Percy's *business*, hey?"

Did he…?

"You're getting less funny by the second," David tells him. "Give me the phone."

"You don't understand," Caolan explains. "I *have* to text Alistair and Andrew. If they find out I knew and didn't tell them, they'll never forgive me. We're bros."

An involuntary laugh bursts from me, even as I pray that David gets the phone away from him. I love Andrew and Alistair. I really, really do. I trust them with my life. But if they get any hint of something happening between me and Brandt, they'll leap headlong into a combined matchmaking/heckling scheme that will make my life a misery.

"You're *bros*?" David says incredulously. "What stupid movie have you been watching? Never mind. Let me put it this way: give me the phone, or you'll need to ask one of your bros to let you sleep in their guest room for the rest of the night."

Caolan gasps.

"On the other hand," David continues, "if you show me how good a friend you can be to Percy right now, we can do—"

"Do I really need to hear this bit?" I interrupt. They ignore me.

"You mean with the—"

"Exactly," David confirms. "What's more important, me naked except for a flight jacket and lightsaber, or your *bros*?"

I wish I hadn't heard that.

"I do want to be a good friend to Percy," Caolan says, wavering. I push aside the perverted *Star Wars* images bombarding my mind and go in for the kill.

"It's not like you'd need to keep it a secret forever," I point out. "When I'm ready for people to know, you can be the one to tell them."

"Really?" he asks hopefully.

"Absolutely."

"Well, that sounds okay. So tell us everything."

I blink. That backfired on me. "Tell you everything about what?"

"You and Brandt. Are you sure you didn't hook up?"

"Very sure," I confirm. "It's not the kind of thing I would have forgotten." I try not to think about how long it's been since I had sex with another person. After I finished up at CSG, I meant to do something about that… get out and meet new people, start dating.

Three years later, I still mean to do it. At least now I have a certain someone in mind. Even if he is currently winging his way to the other side of the continent, soon to be putting an ocean between us.

"What did happen, then?" he asks impatiently. This is not the sober, responsible Caolan I first met. Andrew and Alistair have been a very bad influence on him.

I shrug, even though they can't see it. "Nothing. We flirted a bit, that's all."

"And he asked you to visit," David prompts. "Are you going to? We'd love to see you."

Every atom in me wants to scream *"Yes!"* but instead I say, "Maybe. My lease here is up in a few more weeks, and I miss you all."

"Bet you never thought you'd say that," David says dryly.

"Oh, come on," I protest. "You know I love all of you." He's not wrong, though. Love or not, there were days when I could have cheerfully murdered them all, even him—maybe especially him. I usually had great appreciation for his to-do lists, but once or twice, I may have fantasized about smothering him with them.

"We know. And we all miss you too. Caolan will come and get you whenever you want."

"I will," Caolan agrees. "Right now, if you want. And you're welcome to stay with us, although I'm sure you'll have plenty of options."

"Including Brandt, from the sounds of it," David inserts slyly. "After all, what better way to get to know him? It certainly worked for us."

I snort-laugh, remembering his insistence that he and Caolan were just "friends who fuck," even though Caolan was living with him and had declared his undying love to anyone who would listen. It didn't take long for David to admit he was wrong.

"That's an excellent idea!" Caolan declares. "I'll tell Brandt."

"No!" David and I shout in unison.

"Let Percy handle it," David continues at a lower decibel. "Do not tell Brandt anything."

"Please," I add. Although... maybe it's not a bad idea. I could just show up on Brandt's doorstep with a suitcase and tell him I want to get to know him better. Maybe add a wink so there's no doubt about what I mean.

Knowing my luck, he'd either have someone waiting in his bed or think I meant we should practice trust falls. Which… no. Not ever.

Nope, cautious is the way to go. *If* I decide to pursue this, it will be in a sensible manner.

I groan.

"What's wrong?" David asks.

"I think I'm turning into my father."

"I didn't know that was possible," Caolan marvels. "Is it a shifter thing, or does it happen to all Earth species? Does it happen to everyone, or can you choose?"

"It's not possible," David tells him. "Percy's being dramatic." Then to me, "Why do you think you're turning into your father? Which you're not. There aren't enough sticks in the world to shove up your ass to make you him."

I smile faintly because I know my father would be utterly aghast at that kind of crudity. I hope some part of him can sense what we're saying and his skin is crawling right now. "I was just thinking that I need to be sensible about how I do this with Brandt—if I do—and that's exactly what he would say."

"He sounds boring," Caolan says. "You're not boring. You were the lucifer."

"What he said," David declares before I can think of a response. "Your father would never even contemplate having sex with Brandt or anyone who wasn't properly vetted and willing to comply with his rules and schedule. Wait, are we talking about you and Brandt having sex, or did you want something more long-term?"

I pause. I hadn't thought about that. Would I be interested in more than just sex with Brandt? If it worked out that way, obviously.

"I don't know," I admit. "Sex was what I was thinking about, but…"

There's the sound of hands clapping. "Yes! A relationship plot! And this time I get to be involved."

"What are you talking about?" David asks Caolan.

"No plots," I add. "There will be no plotting." I know exactly what he's talking about.

"Nothing," Caolan says. "No plots. Nothing."

David sighs. "We'll talk about this later. If you're thinking about some kind of asinine matchmaking scheme you and your bros can spring on Percy, forget it."

"It wouldn't be *asinine*," Caolan says in a wounded tone.

"If Alistair's involved, I'm pretty sure it would. Percy, it seems like you've got something to think about, but if I can offer my opinion…?"

"Of course." That's mostly why I called.

"Come for the visit. Have sex with Brandt. And then just see what happens."

I purse my lips. "You really think I should just… sleep with him? Just like that?"

"Well, I'm not going to force you to do it if you don't want to, but if even a small part of you is interested, then yes. I do. He's a charming, intelligent, interesting man, and you've been hot for him since you met."

I make a sound. It might be a squeak.

"Didn't think I'd noticed?" He sounds smug. Insufferable beast.

"There was a lot going on, and you were occupied with Caolan anyway," I reason. "Of course I thought you didn't notice." Hoped. Desperately. At least he didn't say anything to the others. If Andrew or Alistair or Elinor had known… well, there would have been a Relationship Plot, as Caolan put it.

"I was too busy to do anything about it, but I noticed," he affirms. "If things hadn't gone down the way they did, I would have been encouraging you to jump him three years ago."

He means if I hadn't stopped being lucifer. There's always a lot of upheaval when the mantle of power changes over, and then I left, so there was no chance for him to intervene.

"So it's true?" Caolan asks, sounding avidly interested. "You wanted Brandt back then too?"

"I was aware of how attractive he is," I correct, then wince. I really did sound like my father this time. "Yes," I admit, sighing. "But there was so much going on. It didn't seem the right time to act on it."

"You should have. Some things should never be delayed. What if Tish and Éibhear had won? You could have died or been enslaved without ever having fucked Brandt."

I pull the phone away from my ear and stare at it. After all the years I've spent with kooky people, this kind of thing shouldn't surprise me, but it still does.

Even with the phone away from my ear, I can hear David explaining why sex with Brandt probably wouldn't have been a priority concern if I'd been dead or enslaved. I listen, amused, as Caolan counters with the argument that if he'd let potential death and enslavement stop him, they would never have got together.

"Love takes priority over everything else," he declares loftily.

"Yeah, but we're not talking about love; we're talking about fucking," David tells him.

"That should take priority too." Caolan's voice deepens, and I lift the phone back to my ear fast before they can get sidetracked and start their weird *Star Wars* roleplay while I'm still listening.

"Anyway," I say loudly, "that's in the past. It's what to do now that matters."

"Do him," Caolan says baldly, and I can't hold back the snort.

"Charming," I comment.

"He's right, though," David agrees. "If that's what you want, don't let the memories of your father's voice get in the way. Come here, hang out with us for a while, fuck Brandt, and just see where life takes you."

I'm a bit surprised by how Zen David's being about this. He's not usually the "see where life takes you" type. Normally he would have already put together a detailed plan of action with multiple backup and contingency plans. Maybe being with Caolan has mellowed him?

"You've got a plan," I realize. "You've planned me having a fling with Brandt."

"Of course I haven't," he sputters. "Why would you think that?"

"I've known you over four hundred and fifty years, that's why. You planned for this contingency."

Silence.

"Did you?" Caolan asks, sounding… hurt? "David, how could you keep this from me?"

"It's not an *actual* plan," David defends. "I didn't do SMART goals or a timeline or anything. It's just… a very rough outline of steps I could take in the event that the two of you pulled your heads out of your asses."

"And what are those steps?" I ask faintly, trying to remember why David is one of my favorite people in the world. He was the first person I called when I became lucifer, and I've missed him the most of anyone since I left the role. But right now, I would cheerfully set him on fire.

"Well, the first one was getting you and Brandt in the same place again," he admits reluctantly. "Or otherwise engineering a meeting between you."

He wouldn't… "If I find out you had something to do with Benisch—"

"I didn't, I swear. That was just a really weird and fortuitous coincidence."

The only reason I believe him is because I know David would never risk a child. "And the second step?"

He hesitates. "I'm really uncomfortable discussing this."

"Not as uncomfortable as you would be if I was there, ripping your intestines out," I tell him in my sweetest voice.

"No intestine ripping," Caolan warns. "Don't worry, Percy, I'll deal with this. I can't believe you wouldn't let me call my bros *and* warned me off creating a Relationship Plan when you had one all along," he tells David. "I'm heartbroken."

"Caolan, focus. I need to know the next step of the

plan," I insist, though I'm not really sure why. Am I going to follow David's plan, or just muddle through on my own? Or even just pretend none of this happened and go to Indonesia like I intended?

"I'm not telling you," David says. "It's not relevant. You don't have to follow a plan I put together because I was bored and wanted to use my new planning software."

The words are right, but he seems to be forgetting how well I know him.

"So I'll just fumble along by myself—"

"Hopefully Brandt will be there too," he interjects.

"—and you won't interfere at all? No helpful suggestions that might steer me in a certain direction? Like the ones you were making not five minutes ago?"

He sighs. "Percy, I'm sorry. I'm sorry I did this—even though you were never supposed to know. And even though you had no qualms about butting into my love life three years ago. But I promise that if you decide you want to start something up with Brandt, I will not interfere."

I ignore the part about me butting into his love life. It's only partly true—all I did was make some gentle suggestions. Come to think of it, one of them might have been "fuck him and see where it goes."

"Very well. I'll think about this and let you know if I need a place to stay. Caolan, could I impose upon you for transportation to wherever I'm going next?"

"Always," he answers promptly. "But you should know, if it's not here, I'll complain the whole way."

I smile. It's nice to be wanted. "I'll keep that in mind while I'm planning," I promise. We chat for a few minutes more, but I'm very aware of how late it is there and that they have a role play to enact, so I don't keep them, even though it's nice to hear their voices. I should call more often.

Or just go back. A nice long visit would cure me of missing them.

I set my phone on the arm of the chair and sigh, staring out the window. It's baking hot out there, the light bright and harsh, but still it's beautiful. Not my forever place, but I do love it for what it is. I push aside the disappointment that I need to cross one more place off my list. It's a big world. There has to be somewhere perfect for me. And when I find it, I'll find the perfect job or vocation to fill my days, too. I just need to keep looking.

My phone trills a familiar—and dreaded—ringtone, and I close my eyes. I desperately want to send it to voicemail or even block the number completely, but that won't stop him from finding a way to get in touch. I've been avoiding him for a while, so it's probably best to suck it up and listen to him whine for a while so I don't feel like a bad son.

"Hello, Father."

"Where have you been?" he snaps. "I've been trying to reach you for days, Percival!"

I feel my cheek twitch as he uses my full name. Part of the reason I go by Percy is because he's ruined my birth name for me. I can't hear it without flashing back to childhood lectures about proper behavior and living up to the family name.

"Phone service isn't always good here," I tell him. It's mostly a lie. Sure, service is better closer to Broome, and it's nowhere near as good as in the larger cities down south, but I have decent coverage almost all the time.

"Yet another reason you should return to where you belong instead of gallivanting through the wilderness. Where are you?"

I clear my throat to cover my snort of derision. There's no way I'm telling him exactly where I am—he'd send someone to try to bring me back. They'd fail, of course, but it's a hassle I don't want. "I've been moving around," I reply vaguely. "Was there something you needed, Father? How's Mother?"

"She's well, I believe. Busy with social obligations." There's approval and distant fondness in his tone now. My parents are a well-matched pair with high regard for each other's ambitions. They'd have the same for me if I had any ambitions—the fact that I don't feel a driving need to be a merchant banker or corporate lawyer causes them deep disappointment.

And speaking of… "I have a wonderful opportunity for you, Percival," my father continues. "A fellow at my club has an opening in his firm—"

"No, Father," I interrupt firmly. It's best not to let him get properly started. "I'm not interested."

"You haven't even heard what the job is!"

"Still not interested." It could be in any number of fields, since I spent the four centuries before the magic selected me to be lucifer getting an expansive education and then working for a few decades at a time in the related fields. I love learning, and I had fun in a lot of those jobs, but none of them were perfect for me.

"Percival, you can't keep flitting around the world like an itinerant butterfly," he begins. "You have a responsibility to your family name to settle down and contribute to your heritage." I say nothing, and he sighs, changing tack. "Do you truly want to be alone forever? What about children? You know the Kenworthys have a lovely daughter. Or there's a charming incubus your mother wants you to meet. The son of one of her gardening club friends. He's a stockbroker with a very impressive reputation."

I don't know what excites my father more, the thought of grandchildren to continue the family line or a wealthy and connected stockbroker. Either way, he's not using me to get them.

"Thank you, but no," I insist. "But it might interest you to know that I'm thinking of going back to the States and doing some consulting work for CSG." And hooking up with a sexy dragon. But Father definitely doesn't need to know that.

"Consulting for the government," he says in a tone most people reserve for "cleaning slime out of the shower drain." There's a long pause, then he adds, "I suppose that's at least a productive use of time. While you're there, at least consider meeting this stockbroker. Or there's a very influential banker you might like. If you're not going to contribute directly to the family, Percival, you could at least do your duty in other ways."

Yes, that's right, my father wants to pimp me out to strengthen the family heritage. Never mind that for decades I was the leader of our community, selected for the role by the existential magic that makes up every fiber of existence. Dear old Dad considers that only a stepping stone on the path that is "worthwhile contribution" to our family reputation.

"I'll consider it," I concede, just to end the call sooner.

He doesn't need to know my mind is made up—and not just about that, but other things too. I'm going back to the US.

Brandt and I have unfinished business.

CHAPTER FOUR

Percy

It's DREADFULLY COLD. For some stupid reason, I'd forgotten that it's heading into winter in the US, and I'm still wearing the shorts and short-sleeved polo shirt that were very appropriate for an outback summer. And why am I outside anyway? Caolan was supposed to be bringing me back to his and David's place.

He steps through the portal and closes it as I look around. It takes only a second for me to recognize where we are. The terrace at Andrew and Noah's penthouse apartment.

"Forget to mention something?" I ask Caolan, and he shrugs.

"Everybody wanted to see you right away," he explains. "It was easier this way."

"You could have mentioned it." I head toward the glass doors with my suitcases, keen to get out of the cold. "It's not like I wouldn't have come."

I barely have a moment to notice his sudden silence before the doors are opening and people are pouring out.

Noisy people.

Touchy-feely people.

People I adore.

"Inside!" I shout, because that's the only way to be heard over the clamoring voices. "I'm cold."

That's all it takes for them to retreat into the apartment, drawing me with them, divesting me of my luggage and wrapping me in the warmth of their company.

"We missed you!" Sam exclaims, grabbing me in a tight hug. "It's so good to see you." I hug him back, feeling the soothing wash of the lucifer's presence surround me. It's a little weird—for so long, that was me. I was the one whose presence was a reassuring influence over others. It's nice now to be on the receiving end, but at the same time, I do miss having the constant companionship of the magic.

As if it's aware of my thoughts, it brushes over me. It still does visit me sometimes, and it stuck pretty close in those initial weeks after the changeover, but it's really not the same.

I finally make myself let go of Sam. "All good?" I ask, unable to resist. He'd have called if he needed help, I know that, but even after three years I still find myself worrying. *Not your job anymore.*

He smiles reassuringly, and the stroke of comfort brushes against me. "All good. I just missed you. Are you back for good?"

I'm saved from having to answer—it seems David and Caolan have managed to keep some of my secrets —by having a six-foot-five, tank-sized hellhound pounce on me.

"My turn, my turn! Peeeeeeercyyyyy!" Alistair

snatches me into a hug. "How could you have left us for so long? We've been lost and alone without you!"

I snort a laugh against his chest but squeeze him back, breathing in the familiar scent of hellhound. While I've been deliberately picking remote areas to live in during my odyssey, maybe that was a mistake. There are far fewer members of my community in those areas, and I hadn't realized how much I'd missed simple things like the smell of my people.

Then Alistair squeezes me tighter, and I rethink the whole I-missed-him part.

"Can't breathe," I finally gasp, and he lets me go.

I move around the group, getting hugs from everyone—even Gideon. I was expecting more of a pat on the back than a real hug, so it surprised me when he pulled me in close. "It's good to see you," he mutters gruffly. "Sam missed you a lot."

My old team is here, along with their significant others—all except Elinor's fiancé, who has to work. I met him twice before I left, when their relationship was still new, but I've been kept thoroughly in the loop by everyone over the years. The consensus is that we like him because he's in complete awe of Ellie's amazingness.

"Are you here to stay?" she demands, holding my wrists tightly and refusing to let go. She might not be as big as her cousin Alistair, but she's got just as much strength. "Where do you think you'll be in April? If you can't get back here, Javier and I are getting married before you leave again."

There's a chorus of hisses. "Your mother would die if you tried to move the wedding," Alistair predicts.

"And you definitely wouldn't be Gran's favorite anymore. I support this idea."

"Even if I wasn't the favorite anymore, it wouldn't be you," Elinor snaps, then turns back to me. "Percy?"

"I would never miss your wedding," I promise. "As long as Caolan can come and get me, I'll be back from wherever I am. Don't cause trouble with your mum." I know her mother pretty well, and I definitely don't want to be blamed for upsetting the wedding plans.

"So you're not here to stay, then?" Noah asks, and a disappointed murmur runs around the room.

"Probably not." I wiggle my wrists free from Elinor and take a seat on the couch Andrew took six weeks to choose. Oh, not the frame—he picked that in ten minutes. But then he had to decide on upholstery fabric, and apparently there is no being in the known universe pickier than an eight-hundred-year-old vampire.

"Only probably?" says the vampire himself. "What's the deciding factor?"

Damn. I didn't think that through.

"How much you annoy me, and how quickly," I counter, then shiver. It's involuntary, I swear—even inside with the heat on, I'm not dressed for the weather.

They all notice, of course. Most of them are trained investigators. "You should change," David suggests. "We've got food coming any minute, and you don't want your teeth chattering while you're trying to eat."

"Nice tan, by the way," Alistair adds.

"Thank you. It was entirely accidental." I didn't exactly spend a lot of time sunning myself in biped form in the absurd heat.

"Come and use the guest room," Noah says, grabbing one of my suitcases. "You can have a shower to warm up, if you want."

I follow him gratefully, wondering why I ever left. I mean, I know why—I wanted some quiet time for myself, space to get used to the change in my life and maybe discover what my vocation is. I wanted to avoid my father and the unwanted future he has planned for me. Plus, as much as I love all of them, they will very quickly drive me nuts again. But right now, before they've really had the chance to do that, I can't imagine anywhere else in the world I'd rather be.

When I rejoin them ten minutes later, dressed more appropriately and ready to eat the food I heard arrive, I'm met by a sudden silence and all eyes turning my way.

Uh-oh.

I pretend I don't notice as I find a seat and reach for a slice of pizza. It's obvious they were talking about me… the question is, were they merely plotting a way to get me to stay, or have David and Caolan spilled the beans about my other reason for being here? Chewing calmly, I say nothing. One of them will crack soon. My money's on—

"I'm so happy for you!"

—Alistair.

Aidan, his boyfriend and the shifter species leader— my species leader—elbows him hard.

"So happy you're here, I mean," Alistair amends, pouting at Aidan.

I turn a level gaze on David, who holds up his hands. "Not me. They guessed. And then Caolan had to share the details with his bros." He rolls his eyes.

"They *guessed*?" How in the world did they do that?

"It wasn't so much a guess," Noah begins, "as it was a matchmaking scheme. Andrew thought if you hooked up with someone, it might make you stay longer. Brandt seemed like an obvious choice."

I clamp my mouth closed. I really, really want to ask why Brandt is an obvious choice for me to hook up with, but that's a can of worms that could be dangerous. What if David wasn't the only one who'd noticed my, er… fascination with him?

It's okay, though—I don't need to ask. Andrew takes it upon himself to explain anyway.

"He's mature—in age, I mean, which leads to the second benefit, that he's young at heart. You're a serious kind of person, Percy, and you need someone fun to keep you from getting stodgy."

"Thanks." I can't help wincing, but not for the reason they probably all think. Lily used to call me stodgy all the time. I really miss hearing it.

"You and he got along well, he's very attractive, and —this is the most important part—he's the leader of his people."

"Why is that the most important part?" I reach for the wineglass Noah's filling for me. If Andrew's about to say something that makes me seem elitist, I'll know I really have turned into my father.

"Because you need people to look after."

I bobble the glass, spilling wine all over the food. "Shit!"

"Don't worry, everyone knows food is improved by wine," Sam says breezily. "It's only human wine, anyway. Lolly water. Now, that was a very interesting reaction there, Percy."

"It was not," I say, lifting my hand to my mouth to

lick the spilled wine off it, then grabbing the glass and taking a gulp of what's left. Human alcohol may well be like soda to shifter metabolism, but drink enough of it fast enough, and it does have an effect.

"Oh, it was," Andrew insists, leaning forward, his gaze fixed on me and a wicked little smirk on his face. I hate that smirk. "I hit a nerve, clearly."

"You did n—"

"It's fine, Percy," Elinor interrupts. "We all know you're a caregiver at heart. It's part of what made you such a great lucifer. Of course you need people to look after. Brandt would be an amazing match for you, because he comes with five thousand needy dragons."

I just sit there with my mouth open. It's not true. It's not. Didn't I spend the last three years living in remote locations so I wouldn't be surrounded by people who might need me?

And you missed them the whole time, a snarky voice says in the back of my head.

Shoving it away, I say, "I'm not looking for a match. If Brandt and I hook up, it will just be for that. A hookup. I don't want people to look after. I just want sex."

Alistair makes a sound into the sudden silence. He's been suspiciously quiet for the past few minutes— possibly because Aidan is right beside him with a sharp elbow at the ready.

"What?" I ask, resigned to whatever nonsense is going to come out of his mouth. But he surprises me.

"If that's what you want, you should get it."

Gideon coughs. "Did you get hit on the head?"

Ignoring him, Alistair keeps his gaze focused on me. "None of us actually believe you, but if you think you just want sex, well…" He shrugs. "Have sex. With Brandt. Enjoy it."

"Thanks for your permission," I say dryly. "What do you mean, none of you believe me? Why don't you believe me? I'm telling the truth!" Aren't I? I don't really want to get drawn into a proper relationship with a tens-of-thousands-year-old dragon who's responsible for the well-being of all dragonkind, do I? Have people constantly interrupting dinners, quiet evenings at home, sleep, basically every free moment, to dump their problems and beg for help? Spend time attending ceremonies and mediating between factions?

No. Of course not. I had enough of that when I was lucifer.

Liar.

This is about me needing to have sex with more than just my hand and a dildo, and Brandt being a funny, charming, handsome man who makes my hormones sit up and sing. This is about doing something just for me, not about finding a way to once more spend my time doing for other people.

Liar.

I really hate that little voice. Is it my conscience? It needs to sit down and shut up.

Sex. This is about sex with Brandt.

And if it happens to go beyond that—

Oh, fuck.

The one thing I hate more than the voice of my conscience? When it's right.

I TAKE A DEEP BREATH. And then another one.

One more for good luck.

Not because I'm nervous. Why would I be nervous? There's nothing to be nervous about. I always show up at the homes of men I'm attracted to and ask for a shag. This is *ordinary*.

And yet, I'm still sitting in my rental car at the gate.

Would this be easier if Brandt was at his apartment in the city? Should I have waited until the workweek began to approach him there, instead of getting all worked up and defensive about what my friends said and hiring a car on a Saturday morning and driving out to the acreage the dragons own outside the city?

Probably. I would have had less time to think about my impulsive behavior.

What am I even going to *say*? "Hey, wanna fuck?" I don't think I could do that—in fact, a tiny part of me is dying of embarrassment at just the thought. And I didn't even think about the fact that Brandt is not the only one who lives here. The dragons closest to him, who support him in his role as wing leader, also have rooms in what David told me is a "mansion on steroids," and many other dragons come and go at all times. So... essentially I'd be walking in and announcing to all of dragonkind that I want to do their wing leader.

I bang my head against the steering wheel.

What are my options? I can turn around and make the two-and-a-half-hour drive back to David and Caolan's place. David will probably stop Caolan from asking why I'm back so soon, but they'll both *know* something happened—or didn't happen, as the case may be. They'll wonder if I chickened out or if Brandt said *no, thanks*—

Oh crap, I didn't consider that. What if I proposition him and he's not interested?

No. No, that's not going to happen. He made it pretty clear in Australia that he wanted to start something between us. He invited me to come and "get to know him better." Nobody could expect me to think he meant coffee and Twenty Questions, right?

So… options. Go back to the city, wait until Monday, and then visit him at his apartment. Or go back to the city, pretend this whole thing never happened, visit with my friends, then leave for Indonesia.

Or ring the damn gate bell, see Brandt, and tell him what I want.

I do want it. A lot. I'm just not used to asking for sex so plainly. Maybe I need to practice?

"Hey, wanna fuck?" I say out loud, wincing as the words roll off my tongue. Nope. No. Uh-uh. I'll never be able to say that to another person. Maybe if I rephrase it… used a euphemism… "I came to get to know you better."

That's easier to say, but it's so… generic. And what if he does think I mean coffee and Twenty Questions? No, I need to find middle ground. Something that's sexy and clear, but not… crass. I need a classy way to ask Brandt to have sex with me. What's a classy euphemism for sex? I cast my mind back through the years… a popular one when I was much younger was "to ride a dragon upon St. George," but what with him being an actual dragon, that might get confusing.

Ooh, there's an idea… "I want to go for a naked dragon ride."

"I'm afraid we don't offer those here," a stern voice

says, and I shriek and jump, hitting my head on the car door. How the hell could I have been so distracted that I didn't smell or hear someone walk up to the car?

Wait… As I turn my head—my poor, bruised head—toward the window, I still don't smell anything. I can see the man bending down to peer inside, but I can't smell him. At all.

Adrenaline explodes inside me, and I make myself take a deep breath. Then I wind the window down just a few inches. "Are you using some kind of masking spell?"

The part of his face I can see appears startled, then he huffs. "I think the right to ask questions is mine right now. Who are you, and what's your business here?"

I'm pretty sure he's a dragon. It's hard to tell without being able to smell him, since a huge part of shifters being able to recognize other species is through scent, but there's also a sense of otherness that the dragons and elves have, and something about dragon eyes that sets them apart from elves. Either way, I have been sitting here at the gate for a while, and it's not unlikely that someone noticed and came to make sure I wasn't up to no good.

"My name is Percy Caraway, and I'm here to see Brandt," I say, then remember—too late—that this man heard the whole naked-dragon-ride comment. Heat rushes into my face. Well, there goes any chance I had of keeping this quiet.

The dragon leans down further so he can see my face properly, then says, "Oh wow, you are! I'm so sorry, I didn't recognize you in the car."

Huh? Does that mean I could fight crime unrecognized… as long as I stay in the car?

He's still talking, much friendlier now.

"Sorry about sneaking up on you. It wasn't deliberate. I was flying overhead when I saw you sitting here, and I came down fast. I guess the distortion shield hasn't completely dissipated yet."

I make a mental note that the shield also affects smell and sound, which I didn't know before. "Uh, that's fine. I should have been paying more attention, anyway." *No, you idiot! Don't remind him that you were thinking about sex with Brandt!*

"Is Brandt expecting you today? I'm sure he'll be thrilled to see you, but your name wasn't on the visitor list."

Oh crap. Now what?

"Not today specifically," I prevaricate. "But I ran into him in Australia a few weeks ago and said I'd come for a visit."

"Okay, no worries. Let me just call up to the house and get them to open the gate. I can't do it from here, I'm afraid."

"That's fine. Thank you," I manage as he pulls out a cell phone. He doesn't bother trying to keep his voice down for the call, and shifter hearing being what it is, I can hear both sides of the conversation clearly.

"How are you calling when you're supposed to be on aerial surveillance? You better not be shirking!"

"I'm at the front gate. Percy Caraway is here to see Brandt," my companion says.

"Percy Caraway? That name sounds… you mean the previous lucifer?"

"Yes, the previous lucifer."

"What's he doing here? Is he on the list? I don't remember seeing him on the list."

"No, he's not on the list—"

"Are you sure it's him and not somebody pretending to be him?"

"Of course I'm sure it's him. Seriously, you need to stop watching those conspiracy thrillers; you're getting paranoid."

"It's not paranoia when someone might really be conspiring against you. We have a duty to protect Brandt and all dragonkind. It's a calling for which—"

"Yeah, yeah. Are you going to open the gate?"

A sniff. "If he's not on the list, we don't know if Brandt will want to see him."

"Well, *ask him*, then. But I'm pretty sure he'll want to see him." There's just a hint of a leer in that last sentence, and I resist the urge to slam my head against the steering wheel. Instead, I grab my phone and text David while the dragon—shit, I didn't get his name—continues to argue with… the other dragon. The paranoid goody-two-shoes one.

Percy: If a rumor starts going around about me wanting a naked dragon ride, please try to squash it.

It takes literally only seconds for him to text me back.

David: Okay

David: Is it true?

David: Do I even want to know what's happening?

Percy: Probably, but sadly, none of it is interesting. At the gate. Humiliated myself in front of guard. Haven't even seen Brandt yet.

David: I really wish I was there to see this.

Percy: I may need to rethink our friendship

I'm waiting for him to reply when the guard beside me ends the call. I put the phone in the center console and turn my attention to him.

"They're going to open the gate any— There it goes. Drive on up to the house, and someone will show you where to park."

"Thank you," I say, trying to sound grateful for his help and not just terrified that this is a big mistake. "I'm sorry, I didn't get your name."

"I'm Wil, Mr. Caraway. Wilhelm."

"Nice to meet you, Wil. Please call me Percy." I haven't been called Mr. Caraway in more than fifty years, and I wasn't that fond of it back then, either. I've been told that rebellion against one's parents is very common, but where others choose criminal misdemeanors, my rebellion is informality. *Take that, Dad.*

Wil nods and smiles, then backs away from the car, and I start the engine and put the car in gear. Too late to back out now.

I follow the driveway through mostly wooded land. It's fantastic, and my cat purrs contentedly inside me, loving the idea of this space to play in. The trees open into a clearing dominated by—as David said—a house on steroids. It's genuinely huuuuuuge, and my jaw drops at the sight. I was told to expect a megamansion, but this is… wow.

As I approach, a man comes around the side of the house and waves at me, then gestures for me to follow him. I steer in that direction. There are no cars anywhere in sight—although, being able to fly, they probably don't need many—and the driveway does lead that way. Sure enough, there's what looks to be at least a four-car garage, based on the number of doors, along the side of the house and a paved forecourt with plenty of space for parking. Two other cars are parked along the tree line, and I follow the waved directions of my guide and park there also, then turn off the car.

And sit. Because I'm really not sure I can handle getting out of the car right now.

Alas, my reprieve doesn't last long. The light thud of footsteps grows steadily nearer. I suck in a deep breath, then grab my phone and pretend to be absorbed by it. There's a new text from David, but I don't bother opening it. Too late, anyway—my guide has arrived.

He taps lightly on the window. I don't jump this time, thankfully. I think I've made enough of an idiot of myself in front of these dragons for today. So I open the door, and as he steps back to give me room, I get out of the car, pocketing my phone.

"Hi," I say, trying to sound casual and normal as I stick out my hand. "I'm Percy."

The dragon, who manages to be incredibly attractive in a homicidal-looking kind of way, squints suspiciously at me before shaking my hand quickly. Unlike Wil, who was carefully glamoured to look human, this dragon's alien bone structure is clearly visible. The heaviness around the brow and eye sockets, the blade-sharp cheekbones, and the pointed chin are all unmistakably nonhuman, even with his hair covering his ears. Based on the way he's glaring at me, even before he opens his mouth and I recognize his voice, I suspect he's the paranoid conspiracy theorist Wil spoke to on the phone.

"My name is… John. John Smith."

Uh-huh.

I'm not sure why he's fake naming me—unless he thinks I'm going to try to steal his identity?—but I just smile. "Nice to meet you, John. And sorry to crash your weekend. Is Brandt around?"

His dubious glare deepens. "Do you have ID?"

Choking back a laugh, I reach for my wallet, and he scrambles back a few steps, shouting, "Watch it!"

I pause. "I need to get my ID from my pocket," I explain patiently. "Also, you know I'm a shifter, right? I don't need a hidden weapon."

If anything, that makes things worse.

"Are you threatening me?" he demands.

"I'm really, really not," I promise. "Would it make you feel better to get my ID yourself? It's in my wallet, in my back pocket."

He eyes me like I'm a ticking bomb, then says, "Keep your hands where I can see them—and don't even think about shifting," before edging around me. I stand still, eternally grateful that David nor any of my other friends are here to see this, and wonder if anyone else ever had to go through this for sex that they weren't even sure they had the guts to ask for.

My wallet is drawn from my pants pocket, then *John* takes a few steps back and flips it open. He studies the ID—just a standard human driver's license—closely, looking back and forth between it and me for several loooooooong minutes before he grunts, closes my wallet, and tosses it to me. I catch it and tuck it safely away.

"Fine. You can come in. Don't touch anything."

Does he think I'm going to steal the silver? Or break something? Reining in my amusement, I obediently follow him toward the house. We enter through a side door into a spacious mudroom, then go down a hallway. He says not one word the entire time but does keep casting suspicious glances my way. At one point, he stops dead and whirls around suddenly, as if to catch me in the act of… something. It's becoming harder and harder not to laugh at his antics by the time we reach a lovely little sunroom. The entire exterior wall is paned glass, and the room is warm and flooded with light.

"Wait here," he orders. "I'll know if you leave this room."

I smile serenely and take a seat in a lovely wingback chair upholstered in soft, luxurious velvet. "If you take too long, I might have a nap," I warn, and he sniffs before backing out and closing the door.

I never knew tormenting dragons could be so much fun.

The problem is, now that I don't have John Smith's antics to distract me, I'm back to thinking about my reason for being here. I'm in Brandt's house. He's likely to come through that door any minute—assuming John actually tells him I'm here. What am I going to say? Do I chicken out and make up some excuse? I could text David or Sam right now, and they would give me a reason for needing to be here… of course, they would then never let me live it down. Or I could just say I'm back in the States for a visit and decided to come for a drive and see the new dragon headquarters.

Or I could grow a spine and tell him I want a naked dragon ride. Only not in those words.

There's a loud crash somewhere in the house, followed by several thuds and then the sound of running footsteps. Alarmed, I get to my feet, trying to hear what's going on, but there doesn't seem to be widespread panic. Just one person running… down some stairs, maybe? And now along a corridor. The footsteps are getting closer and closer, right near—

The door bursts open, and Brandt practically falls into the room. His wild-eyed gaze lands on me.

"You came!" He lunges forward, then stops so suddenly, I almost look for a string. "I mean… it's so good to see you. Welcome to Draighaimaz."

I turn the last word over in my head. My elvish is terrible still, but I think it translates as "Dragons' Place" or "Dragons' Home," which is lovely. "Thank you," I say politely. "What I've seen of the property is gorgeous, including the mudroom. And this room is just lovely."

He blinks. "The mudroom? Didn't you come in through the front?"

I shake my head. "No, we used the side entrance— which is good, because it's nice and close to where I parked my car." I don't know why I even mentioned the mudroom—probably these stupid nerves—but I definitely don't want to get anyone in trouble, and honestly, that mudroom was nicer than a lot of bedrooms I've been in. When I finally settle down somewhere and find my own home, I'm ripping off the design.

"I suppose that makes sense," Brandt concedes. "But didn't Steffen offer you a tour?"

"Steffen?" I ask innocently, unable to resist. "I haven't met Steffen. Just Wil, at the gate, and John Smith."

For a second, Brandt looks confused, then realization dawns and he laughs, shaking his head. "I need to cancel all those crime streaming services," he mutters. "And maybe put some kind of parental lock on his computer. Was he terribly rude to you?" The exasperated indulgence in his tone tells me John—Steffen—has done this before.

"Not at all. Perhaps overly cautious. And someone with a shorter temper than mine might have been tempted to punch him in the face," I admit, and Brandt snorts.

"Everyone has been tempted to punch Steffen in the face at one time or another. It's his special gift." His smile now is warm and slow and genuine. "I'm so very glad you're here."

All my nerves and tension melt away. I was so stupid to be worried about this… about him not wanting me after all. I take a small step forward. "Me too. I—"

I'm interrupted by thunderous footsteps racing down the hall, accompanied by a shout of "Is it truuuuuue?" A moment later, a familiar face appears in the doorway, so hyperfocused on Brandt that he doesn't notice me standing only a few feet away. "Grandfather, is it true that Percy came here for a naked dragon ride?"

Kill. Me. Now.

How… *how* did the news spread this fast? Isn't Wil supposed to be airborne right now, not sharing gossip? And why could the universe not cut me a break and have him forget all about it?

Brandt, eyes wide, gestures in my direction. Dustin's gaze tracks toward me, then his face lights up. "Percy! You're here!" He races over and grabs me in a tight hug. "It's so good to see you again."

I hug him back, a little surprised. We never really had a hugging kind of relationship. In fact, I really don't know him that well—although I suppose having been through everything that happened together, there's a bond between us. I'm certainly very fond of him.

"It's good to see you too," I say, then draw back. "What have you been up to?" The last time I saw him, he was still acting as a liaison between elf and dragon civilians and CSG—a nonthreatening point of contact people could ask questions of while assimilating into Earth society. David told me a few months back that the job wound down as people became more comfortable in their new environment and the elf and dragon government established itself.

He shrugs, looking utterly adorable. I'm certain he's several millennia old, but for a dragon, that's the equivalent of our early twenties, and he seems to have adopted the dress code of a college student. "I'm taking some time to think about my options," he says. "I started college this year, but I don't know… I think I might defer next semester."

"You what?" Brandt asks, and Dustin's face goes pink. "When did you decide this?"

"It's not decided for sure yet," he prevaricates. "I'm thinking about it."

The set of Brandt's mouth reminds me that Dustin has a reputation for being flighty—and with dragons, that's really saying something, since none of them are particularly staid. Before he can say anything else, though, Dustin throws me under a bus.

"So, is it true? Are you two hooking up? And is 'naked dragon ride' a euphemism, or are you really going to do that? How would it work? I mean, technically we're always naked in our dragon forms… and we're a lot bigger. The logistics might not be ideal."

Yeah… he just said that. Any chance that Brandt might have missed it the first time is now lost.

"Naked dragon ride? It's a euphemism," Brandt says with complete aplomb. "Biped form the whole time." He smirks in my direction, one eyebrow quirked as if to say, "Unless you have other ideas." I shake my head vehemently. I'm pretty sure having sex with him in his dragon form would rip me apart. Have you seen how big dragons are? A barely adolescent one *crushed my shed*. The full-grown adults… well, commercial airplanes are smaller.

I frown. Come to think of it, I don't think I've ever seen a dragon schlong. Admittedly, I haven't seen that many dragons in shifted form, but surely if they're built proportionately, it should have been highly visible.

"Then it's true?" Dustin persists, and Brandt shrugs and looks at me.

"Are you actually asking if I came here to have sex with your grandfather?" I prevaricate. "Don't you think that might be crossing some boundaries?" I'm not going to confirm to Dustin that I'm here for sex when I haven't even discussed it with Brandt yet. Although I guess this puts paid to any idea I might have had about making up a lie and chickening out.

Dustin looks confused. "Boundaries?"

"Go somewhere else," Brandt tells him. "Percy and I need to talk."

Dustin's face lights up. "Ohhhhhh… *talk*. Sure. I'll just… go and… uh…" He backs toward the door. "I'll make sure nobody interrupts you."

I have a sneaking suspicion he plans to listen at the door. Which… creepy.

"Don't worry about that. Go far away. Or we could always talk about college," Brandt threatens, and Dustin moves faster.

"Sorry, gotta run! Byeeeee!" He dashes down the hall. Brandt turns back to me and opens his mouth to say something, but the faint murmur of voices catches our attention. They're speaking softly and quite some distance away, but shifter hearing is acute.

"...doing?" asks a voice I don't know. Maybe Steffen?

"They're... talk," Dustin says, then giggles. "Stay... case he... mad."

"...naked... ride?"

My face flames. I can't believe I'm actually that unlucky. The *one time* I try to coach myself by saying things out loud, someone had to overhear me. And no, it couldn't have been something generic like "you can do it" or even "you're a whiny twat," it had to be "I want to go for a naked dragon ride."

Lily would have died laughing if she was here. But she would also have been so proud—she always told me I needed to be more spontaneous.

I miss her.

I'm snapped out of my thoughts by Brandt closing the door. He leans against it and studies me. "If we keep our voices down, we can probably manage a private conversation," he suggests, and I nod.

"Thank you. I, uh... I'm a little embarrassed," I admit, and he grins.

"I can tell. I think it's adorable."

Adorable? I am *not* adorable. I am a distinguished, powerful man!

"And now you're all miffed... like an adorable kitten." He sounds delighted, and I seriously consider punching him in the face. Doesn't he remember that I used to lead all members of the Community of Species? That I ripped out the throat of my enemy and saved the day? I am *not* adorable. I am a... a... motherfucking badass!

Except even saying that in my head makes me want to cringe. It's such a *bold* statement. Maybe I'd be better off calling myself a competent, capable person instead.

I clear my throat. "Well, all that aside, I'm sorry if my arrival here causes you any inconvenience." Is that the voice of my father coming from my mouth? Why, I believe it is. What is *wrong* with me? I'm known for being a great diplomat. Why can't I say anything right?

"I want to have sex," I blurt. "With you. Obviously. That's why I'm here. For us to… you know. And I'm sorry about the naked dragon ride comment. I didn't mean for anyone to… well, anyway. Oh, and definitely it was a euphemism. Biped sex only. Please. If that's okay." I give up and take a step toward the door, determined to flee this place and leave the scene of the crime far behind me. Murder my own dignity? Check!

The only problem with this plan is that Brandt is still standing in front of the door. No, scratch that, he's now moving toward me, a sly little smile on his handsome face.

"Would anybody believe me if I told them what a stuttery mess you are right now?" he murmurs, stopping right in front of me. If I breathe deeply enough, our chests will touch. The thought sends a shudder through me.

"Probably not," I concede. "I'm generally considered to be quite the statesman."

"I like this Percy better," he whispers, leaning in. "But just for me. My own private Percy—"

I rise on my toes and kiss him. Partly to shut him up, but mostly because I want to. So bad. And it's definitely the right decision.

It starts out bumpy, since Brandt is *still talking*, but

then he shuts up and turns all his focus to the kiss. Ever been kissed by a thirty-thousand-year-old dragon? No? You absolutely must try it. His lips are soft, but the pressure is firm, and he takes charge like nobody's business, hauling me close and bending me back over his arm. It puts me off-balance, reliant on him to keep me from falling, and never before have I realized how much I wanted to give up control. Not until this very moment, when Brandt takes it from me and leaves me to trust that he can keep me upright and feed all my needs.

And he does.

We don't break the kiss until my hormones get the best of me and I moan loudly, squirming against him in an attempt to get some friction on my cock. He sets me back on my feet, then leans down and presses his cheek against mine. He's warm and big and we're both silent, panting slightly as we try to catch our breath.

"So," I say, breaking the silence. My voice is hoarse, so I pull away and clear my throat. "You're interested, then?"

He huffs a laugh. "Very interested. In fact, I'd sweep you up to my bedroom right now, but—"

"They're going to go to Brandt's room! Move!" someone hisses in the hallway.

"—but it's unlikely we would have much privacy," he finishes smoothly, shaking his head as I chuckle. He raises his voice. "We can hear you, and if you don't behave, Percy won't stay!"

I cock my head, listening to the scramble of feet as whoever's out there—at least three people, I think— races away. "I wouldn't have thought that threat would work," I muse. "I mean… is it really a punishment for *them* if you don't get to have sex?" And if it is, dragons are even weirder than I thought.

"They like you," he says. "And they don't want me to be lonely. They've been halfheartedly matchmaking for more seasons than I can count."

Ah. I swallow. "About that."

He tips his head and smiles inquiringly. "About what? The matchmaking? Don't worry, they never found anyone right for me, and I'll tell them to stop now."

"Ha ha. No. Well, yes, but… er." I did not foresee this. I was so busy panicking over how to proposition Brandt that I didn't spend any time thinking about how to tell him I'm not interested in a relationship.

But does he really think I am? And even if he does, well, it's not likely to work out, is it? He's a millennia-old dragon responsible for the safety and well-being of his dwindling people, and I'm an almost-middle-aged shifter trying to find himself and skive off any responsibility that might try to find me. Which reminds me, I need to make sure David and the others know that if my father calls, they have no idea where I am.

I shake my head slightly, trying to focus on the matter at hand, and Brandt frowns. "You don't want me to tell them to stop? I guess we could… I just didn't think you'd be interested in a polygamous relationship. Or did you want to try a throuple—"

"No!" No, that's definitely not for me. I can barely bring myself to ask *one* man to sleep with me—how would I manage two? And the possessive streak I didn't know I had doesn't like the idea of Brandt going from my bed to someone else's, so poly's out too. "No, I didn't mean that. Sorry. I was thinking of something else and trying to clear my head. Please absolutely do tell them to stop matchmaking for you."

He smiles and bends to kiss me again, and I melt into it like butter in the microwave.

What did I just do? Did I… agree to be monogamous with Brandt?

How did that happen?

Brandt pulls away. "You're thinking."

I blink. "Well… yes."

"You shouldn't be thinking while we're kissing." He pouts. "Clearly I'm doing something wrong."

I can't resist leaning up to gently bite his pouty lower lip. "I'm sorry," I murmur, marveling at how comfortable and yet insanely tingly I feel in his arms. "You're not doing anything wrong. I'm just distracted by them" —I wave vaguely in the direction of the door—"and also by wondering how many throuples and poly relationships you've been in."

He shrugs. "A few. There's not much I haven't tried. But I've also been in many, many monogamous couples. It all depends on the person and the situation."

I lean my forehead on his shoulder. "Maybe you can teach me some new tricks," I mutter. My sex life hasn't ever been wild and adventurous. I don't think I'm ready for anything too kinky, but a spice level above vanilla might be nice. Maybe cinnamon—or ginger.

Not any of the peppers, though. That's a little too spicy for me. In the bedroom, I mean. I quite like a lot of spice in my food.

Thank goodness nobody (Brandt) can hear what I'm thinking right now. That would be an embarrassment I'd never come back from.

"You're warm," I say, lifting my head as I realize how very toasty he is.

He nods, clearly amused by my inability to stay on topic, but not in a way that makes me feel bad. Instead, I feel like he's... delighted by me? It's nice.

"Yes. In biped form, we regulate our own body temperature, remember? I like to be warm."

I think I was told that at some point, but I'm too busy processing what it will actually mean for me in my life to try to remember by whom and when. "Oh my, you're going to make the best bedmate!" Especially now that winter is setting in. Ooh, maybe I can convince him to join me on a trip to see the Northern Lights. I've only been once, centuries ago, and it was so damn cold I barely saw anything before holing up in my cabin under a pile of blankets by the fire for the rest of the trip. I would really love the chance to see them properly, and with Brandt standing beside me as my own personal furnace, that could happen.

"I like the sound of that," he says. "We'll spend a lot of time in bed, then. Snuggling."

I think I just invited myself for a sleepover. I am really *bad* at this whole no-strings sex thing, and we haven't even had sex yet.

But I do like snuggling.

I clear my throat, pushing away the thought of snuggling with big, warm, naked, hard-all-over Brandt. Whew. It's getting a little too hot in here now. "Uh, if they"—I wave again toward the door—"are unlikely to give us much privacy, how…?"

He shrugs. "They're like babies. Shiny distractions attract them," he says seriously. "If we disappear upstairs now, in the middle of the day, they'll all be straining their ears to listen. But bedtime tonight? That's ordinary. They'll probably even forget we're here."

That's fucked-up in so many ways, but I'm not going to offend him by saying so.

"And if I put up a privacy spell now, they'll all notice and be waiting for me to take it down so they can tease us," he adds. "But privacy spells at night are common. They won't even notice then."

Okay, that part makes me feel better. I really wasn't looking forward to having however many dragons are here listen to me have sex with their leader. Talk about performance anxiety.

"I guess we wait for tonight, then. I'd like to get to know your people better before they ask me questions about my favorite positions and sexual stamina," I joke, and he laughs.

"May I give you a tour of the house and grounds?" he offers. "We can bring your bag in as well, then have lunch. There's some entertainment planned for this afternoon."

"What kind of entertainment?" I ask curiously, then realize "I don't have a bag." Oh my goodness… I didn't bring a bag. I was so wrapped up in the idea of proving my friends wrong and coming here to proposition Brandt with a just-sex hookup that I didn't bother to pack an overnight bag.

Also… I proved my friends right and have now seemingly embarked on more than a one-night stand with Brandt. I'm never going to live any of this down. Ever. In my life.

I groan. The end of it sounds kind of like a sob.

"It's okay!" Brandt hurries to assure me, looking alarmed. "We have spares of everything here. I'm sure we can find you some toiletries and a clean shirt and underwear."

If only that could fix things. "No, that's not it. I mean, thank you. I appreciate that. I guess I was so eager to get here that I didn't think things through properly." His smile returns, this time a little smug. Since I just admitted I raced out here to shag him without worrying about any of the practicalities, I guess he has a right to be smug. "It's more that when my friends hear how… unprepared I was, it's going to become the butt of all their jokes for a long, long, very long time. Hellhounds do not know when to let a joke go."

"Well, I won't tell them if you don't," he says, then winks. I've always thought winking is either silly-looking or creepy, but Brandt manages to make it sexy. I suddenly understand the old joke about throwing panties for a wink. Would Brandt like me to throw my panties at him?

Oh my goodness, he's going to see my panties. Shit. Shit shit shit. I really didn't think this through. If I had, I would have put on ordinary boxer briefs this morning. But I wanted a confidence boost, so instead I'm wearing a lovely pair of red panties with soft lace trim—never mind that the thing I wanted confidence for would mean taking off my pants!

"Percy?" He's back to looking concerned again, and no wonder. I've been a flaky mess of emotions since I got here, not at all my usual self.

"It's fine," I assure him. "You're right. They never have to know. Thank you." I'll just sneak into a bathroom at some stage and take off my underwear. Commando is fine. I've done that before… I think. I must have at some stage, right? I just can't call up the memory right now.

Never mind that. Time to show Brandt that I'm definitely worth his time and effort, or he's going to back out and this trip and all the worry are going to be wasted. Not to mention, now that I've started anticipating it, I'm very much looking forward to a naked dragon ride.

CHAPTER FIVE

Brandt

PERCY VISIBLY PULLS himself together while I watch. I'm not sure what it is that's been bothering him on and off since he arrived, but hopefully once he's settled in and relaxed a bit, he'll share it with me. I want to solve all his problems and snuggle him and feed him and fuck him through the mattress. And then let him fuck me through the mattress. Is he into that? I hope so.

"Tour?" I offer again. I can find him clean clothes for tomorrow later. It's not like he's going to need pajamas or anything… although now that I'm thinking about it, I wouldn't mind seeing him in one of my shirts and nothing else. My cock stirs at the thought.

"A tour would be lovely," he says, smiling brightly. "And did you say something about entertainment?"

I did, but I regret it. I want to keep him here, not chase him away in horror. A lot of people don't really "get" dragon entertainment, and I'd like at least one night with him before he flees for his life.

"Yes, but that's later. Let me show you the house first." I usher him to the door and then out into the hallway, raising my voice to call, "I can hear you breathing." I can't, actually, but there's a flurry of hisses and footsteps as my beloved housemates scurry out of their hiding places. Percy chuckles.

"You dragons really are just like hellhounds—only bigger, with the ability to breathe fire and fly." His smile turns somewhat vicious. "This must be killing them."

I think I like this vindictive side of him. "The hellhounds?" I check, and he nods. "They were a bit miffed to begin with, but then they got caught up in showing us all the glories of Earth, and now they just like having people to play with. Especially people who can fly and breathe fire. Aidan and I had to ban a few things," I admit.

"That's normal," he says dismissively. "Every time new technology appears, we have to ban hellhounds from using it in some weird manner the inventor never considered. Microwaves, for example." He shudders. "We finally implemented a law stating goods can only be used in the manner described in the manufacturer's manual. That helped, but not everything has a manual."

"Like dragons. Someone—and nobody's saying who —concocted a game called firedive."

He stops in the middle of the hallway and turns to me. "I don't know what that is, but I'm guessing it has something to do with diving through fire?"

I snort. "Yes. It seems they used all their creativity on the game and had none left for the name. It's exactly how it sounds—a hellhound rides a dragon"—for some reason, he goes bright red—"then, midflight, the dragon breathes fire and the hellhound dives off right through it."

The hectic color drains from his face. "Midflight? But hellhounds can't fly!"

"Exactly. The challenge was for the hellhound to make it through the flame unscathed and then be caught by the dragon, who would swing back around. As I understand it, they had to be caught by claws, not just allowed to land on dragonback." I allow myself a brief, wistful thought about how much fun it would have been to have a turn. That kind of precision flying has always been a favorite of mine. But I'm responsible now, and there was no option other than to ban the game. Especially after the number of broken bones.

"Was anyone seriously hurt?" Percy asks, and I shake my head. From the aghast look on his face, he's not thinking it would have been epic to try.

"Oh, no. Nobody ever hit the ground, but there were a lot of bumps and bruises, broken bones, and burns. That kind of midflight maneuvering is tricky, especially with trees and buildings around. Don't tell Sam and King Raðulfr, though. Aidan and I have managed to keep it from them so far."

A half-resigned, half-relieved expression crosses his face. "It's done now," he concedes. "And it sounds like it was a real bonding experience between dragons and hellhounds."

I'm laughing as we emerge from the hallway into the entrance hall. I love this not-a-room room. It stretches up four stories, to an incredible skylight in the pitched roof, and is overlooked by galleries on the two floors above. Only the attic is closed off from it.

"Wow," Percy says, looking up. "Really, wow. This is incredible."

I beam with pride. Truthfully, I decided this was the

property for us the second I saw this space. It's just lucky that the rest of the house and grounds were suitable.

A huge fireplace, the mantel at Percy's head height, dominates one wall. The fire is lit, but mostly for ambiance. Being able to control our own temperature means that dragons don't really care what the weather's like.

"Are you cold?" I ask Percy, belatedly realizing he *can't* regulate his internal temperature and might need help. "Come and stand by the fire. This place has central heating—I just need to find someone who knows how to work it." Maybe Dustin. Steffen certainly knows —he makes it his business to know everything—but it seems he's still not sure about Percy, and I wouldn't put it past him to make it too hot, or blast cold air, or just tell me it's not working at all.

"I'm not cold," he assures me. "Although the fire is lovely. We shifters tend to run warm, so the house feels perfect right now."

I make a mental note to ensure the central heating is up and running before winter sets in properly. If I want Percy to spend time here—a lot of time—I can't freeze him all day.

I'm not worried about keeping him warm at night. He can borrow all the heat he needs from me.

We stand by the old stone hearth, enjoying the heat from the fire and talking about the house's origins.

"This stone"—I lay my hand on the fireplace surround—"is from the fireplace and foundations of the original stone cottage that stood here."

He eyes the stone, which peters off into timber and plaster about fifteen feet up the wall, then looks back at me. "I'm guessing the cottage was considerably smaller than the current house."

"Just a little bit. The way it was told to me, the cottage had been here since—" I pause to make sure I get it right. I'm still not entirely used to the way the Earth species measure time. "—the late 1700s." I peek at his face to see if I've gotten it wrong, but it must make sense. "The original owner was a wealthy man who wanted a home in the woods to vacation in. The house was small compared to this, but actually very comfortable—and I'm told large—by standards then. It was passed down through the family, renovated several times, had plumbing and electricity added, and then was inherited by… hold on, let me remember how the agent described him." This time, my pause is mostly for effect. "He was a 'useless big-city moron who couldn't count to five with his fingers to help him.' There was some other stuff, too, but I don't like to repeat it when *people are listening*."

Instead of scattering again, someone—who sounds like Kethe—yells back, "If you don't want us to listen, stop talking!"

Percy bites his lip, grinning, and I roll my eyes. "Come out here, then, and meet Percy."

This time, there's a definite rush of footsteps—from all over the house. Even those who hadn't been clustered halfway down the hall are coming to cluster around us.

Five eager dragons hovering, studying Percy closely.

This was a bad idea. He's going to run away for sure.

However, Percy seems completely at ease—more so than when it was just the two of us in the sunroom. He smiles genially, radiating that serenity I remember most about our first meeting. It was such a comfort back then, when everything was falling apart around us and we were losing our home, to be in his presence and just feel like everything might be okay. Even if it wasn't, it would be, because Percy was in control.

"Hello," he says. "It's so nice to meet you all."

"Probably because you haven't met them yet," I counter dryly. "Believe me, the feeling of niceness passes."

Kethe boos, a nasty habit she's picked up since moving here. "We're always nice," she protests.

"And Percy already knows me," Dustin adds. "Clearly the niceness lingers!"

"Everyone," I begin, ignoring them, "this is Percy Caraway, my guest." There are a few snickers, one muttered "Yeah, *guest*," and some kissy noises.

Before the heckling can begin and I murder my beloved housemates, Percy steps forward.

"And I also know John," he says innocently, tiddling his fingers at Steffen, whose eyes widen. "Hi, John."

All heads slowly turn toward Steffen.

"John?" Kethe says.

"John Smith," Percy supplies helpfully.

"John Smith," Fabian repeats. "Isn't there a movie with that name?"

We all stare blankly at him.

"You know, the one about the homicidal man and his dog?"

"That's *John Wick*," Dustin corrects.

"There's a movie about a homicidal dog?" Kethe asks. "Is it a shifter?"

"No, just an ordinary dog," Fabian tells her.

"And the dog's not homicidal," Steffen adds. "The man is. Because he loved the dog."

"Loving the dog made him homicidal?" Kethe shakes her head. "I thought pets were supposed to be a calming influence. Maybe I should join one of your movie nights."

"If you want to watch a movie about a homicidal dog, try *Cujo*… or *Man's Best Friend*," Percy suggests, still in that helpful tone that makes me highly suspicious. Dustin whips out his phone to make a note.

"What I want to know," Fabian interjects, "is why Steffen was impersonating a homicidal movie character. Should we be worried?"

Once again, all eyes turn to Steffen. I fold my arms over my chest, looking forward to this.

"I wasn't impersonating a homicidal movie character," he huffs.

"You told Percy that your name was John Wick," Kethe counters.

"I said it was John Smith!"

"Who's John Smith?" Fabian asks nobody in particular. "If you're going to impersonate someone, it should be someone whose name we know. What's the point, otherwise?"

"The point is to remain anonymous so big brother can't hack all my personal information and wipe out my identity for refusing to comply with their demands!" Steffen exclaims.

"I think you've mixed up your conspiracy movies," Percy points out. "There seem to be a few different plots in there."

Steffen squints at him. "You're doing this. You've

turned my own friends against me, isolating me, and now you'll move in for the kill."

"We're not against you," Sophie protests, speaking up for the first time. "Why would we be against you? And why would Percy kill you? I thought he came here to fuck Brandt."

"Hey!" Kethe exclaims.

Sophie looks around. "What? That's what 'naked dragon ride' means, right? Dustin said that's what it meant." She turns to Percy. "I, for one, am very glad you're here. I think Brandt might be getting cobwebs *down there*."

I sputter. The conversation just took a turn I don't like. "There are no cobwebs! Why would you think that?"

"You haven't been with anyone since we came here," she points out. "That's a long time. A spider can build a full orb web in one hour."

My jaw drops. "One hour? Are you sure?" I walked into a full orb web once, the last time I visited Earth before the travel ban, and those things are intricate. How could one tiny spider make the whole thing in an hour?

Sophie nods. "I read it on the internet, and it seemed too fast to be true, so I went into the woods and watched some spiders for a while and used my phone to time it."

"Is that what you were doing when you disappeared for three days?" Kethe asks. "I wondered why you came back looking like you'd been buried."

"I *was* buried," Sophie tells her. "I had to be inconspicuous so the spiders would go about their business, so I buried myself in leaf litter and dirt."

Percy opens his mouth, closes it, then opens it again and says, "For three days?"

She nods. "It took that long."

"You're a dedicated observer," he says, and she beams.

"Thank you."

"See!" Steffen exclaims. "See! There! He's drawing you over to his side with his wiles!"

Dustin reaches over and smacks Steffen in the back of the head. "Stef, I know Percy. Grandfather knows Percy. He's not here to kill you; he's here to clear out the cobwebs with a naked dragon ride."

Percy sighs. "That seems to be catching on. Lucky me," he mutters.

"There are no cobwebs," I say loudly. "I have a perfectly good pair of hands *and* a collection of toys. Believe me, no cobwebs."

Dustin screws up his face. "I could have lived without knowing that."

I throw up my hands. "But you're okay with knowing why Percy's here?" Who knew kids today were so prudish?

Steffen eyes Percy warily. "You're really not here to infiltrate us?"

"Infiltrate what, exactly?" Kethe asks Sophie, who shrugs.

"Could that be a euphemism?" Fabian asks. "Like… *infiltrate*." He leers.

Kethe looks at him. "Go stand on the other side of Steffen," she orders, pointing. He opens his mouth to protest, but she raises an eyebrow and he closes it again and obeys. Nobody wants to piss off Kethe. She rules this place.

"I'm not here to infiltrate you," Percy promises, and I think it's a really good sign that he hasn't already fled screaming. Most people are at least attempting to come up with an excuse to leave by this point. Except the hellhounds, who fit right in. "I just came to see Brandt."

Steffen stares him down for a moment longer, but then the suspicion on his face clears. "Steffen," he says, holding out a hand. "My name's Steffen."

Percy shakes his hand. "It suits you much better than John," he says, then looks around the group, still smiling. "And I know Dustin, of course."

Kethe steps forward, as I knew she would. "I'm Kethe. I run the house and prepare meals. Do you have any food allergies or preferences I should know about?"

Percy shakes his head. "No, thank you. It's lovely to meet you, Kethe. I imagine you have your hands full here." His gesture takes in the immensity of the entrance hall, and I suddenly wonder how Kethe keeps it clean. She's never asked me for a ladder or anything, but there are definitely no cobwebs—hah!—in sight.

Kethe smiles approvingly. "I manage. Let me know if you need anything while you're here. There are always snacks in the kitchen." She looks him up and down and purses her lips. "I know you felid shifters are smaller than us, but have you been eating right?"

"Kethe," I say, resigned. Sex with Percy is never going to happen. We haven't even gotten to lunch yet and he's already been accused of infiltrating us for nefarious, possibly homicidal, purposes, had his personal life shared as salacious gossip, and now been called puny. Just imagine what the afternoon will bring!

"Don't 'Kethe' me. It's my job to look after every single being under this roof, including your afternoon delight, and nobody will ever be able to say I haven't done it."

"Afternoon delight?" Fabian asks. "Is that like Turkish Delight?"

"No," we all say at the same time. Fabian looks put out to be the only one not in the know.

"Well, what is it, then?" he demands.

Percy makes a strangled sound. "You all certainly picked up local slang quickly," he says faintly.

Sophie shrugs. "It's been three years. We measure time in years now, too. I only forget sometimes."

"I forget all the time," Fabian adds. "What's afternoon delight?"

"Sex," Dustin says. "In the afternoon, obviously." My grandson rolls his eyes. "Maybe we should worry about your sex life, Fabian."

"Maybe," Fabian agrees. "It's gotten kind of slow lately. I only had sex six times last week."

Silence falls as we all stare at him.

"*Six*," Steffen sputters. "Six times? With whom? You're single!"

Fabian shrugs, apparently unaware of the effect his bombshell has had. "I know. I think that's part of the reason for the slow patch. It's such an effort to go out and find someone, you know? I tried using one of those apps, but it's hard to know if I'm attracted when I can't use my magic to sense them."

None of us know what to say.

No, wait. I do.

"Good for you, Fabian! We should try to organize a singles group in the area. Make it easier for you to meet people."

"Uh," Percy says.

"Really? That would be great. I kind of miss sex."

He should try using only his hand and some toys for a few cycles—sorry, years—and then see how much he misses sex. Part of me wants to smack him right now.

"We could host it here," Kethe says thoughtfully. "Not always, but sometimes. And we have plenty of room for anyone who wants to stay over."

"Uh," Percy says.

"Maybe we should charge a small fee," Dustin suggests. "Just to cover costs for the hosts."

"Great idea," Fabian declares.

"*Not* a great idea," Percy bursts out, and we all look at him. "Sex parties are one thing, but when you charge money for people to meet up and have sex, it makes you a pimp. Which is not legal here. The last thing you need is human police raiding the estate."

Hmm. I weigh the pros and cons. "Would it really be pimping if neither party having sex gets paid?"

Percy stares at me. "Are you really going to argue about the definition of 'pimp'? Because you could always give that a shot in *human court*. Right after the *human* police get a warrant and search this property. Of course, it might not get to court. Depending on what they find, you might instead get a visit from one of the human security agencies or their military. If you're lucky, CSG will be able to step in before they take you all to some secret lab."

"What kind of secret lab?" Steffen asks immediately. He turns to me. "Did you know this sex group was going to get us strapped to tables and experimented on?" Before I can answer, he whirls on Fabian. "Are you colluding with the enemy?"

"No!" Fabian exclaims, then adds, "I don't think. Who's the enemy?"

"Nobody's colluding with the enemy," Percy soothes. "That was just an example, Steffen. I apologize; I didn't mean to concern you. As long as you're all careful not to attract attention—which charging for sex would certainly do—there's no reason for the humans to suspect you're different from them." He pauses. "Well, not many reasons," he amends.

"And we don't have any enemies," I assure Fabian. I'm pretty sure we don't, anyway.

"Does this mean no sex club?" Kethe asks. "That's a shame. I was looking forward to it."

I look at Percy. If it was up to me, the sex club would be all systems go, but he knows more about what's appropriate here on Earth. The community of species spent nine thousand years hiding from humans—it would be really rude of us to out them after only three years here. Not to mention bad for our own safety. It's nice to have someone right here on hand to point out the problems with exciting ideas. I've gotten better at seeing flaws as I get older, but like most dragons, I still tend to get swept away by thrilling concepts. Usually I rely on Raðulfr for perspective—he's been a king for a long time, and elves aren't generally as fun as dragons, so he always points out the problems.

Maybe if Percy sticks around, I won't need to call the elf king as much.

"A social group for singles—*not* just for the purpose of sex—is fine, as long as you're not charging people. It'll probably end up being unofficially a sex club. But maybe don't market it that way. This area is pretty liberal, but there are probably some strict conservatives who would love to cause trouble for you."

"Oh, oh, I have a question!" Dustin waves his hand. I squint at him. For a short time when we moved here, he was incredibly responsible. I truly thought he was beginning to mature, and I was so proud of everything he was achieving. But since things settled and he was no longer needed as civilian liaison, he's gone back to being flaky, even for a dragon.

"You don't need to wait for permission to ask, Dustin," Percy says, that tiny, amused smile back.

Dustin lets his arm flop to his side. "It's about sex," he announces, and Percy's eyes widen and dart to me. I shrug. Dustin and I had the sex talk a long time ago—well before Percy was even born. I'm well aware that he's sexually active, and he's never been shy about that before.

Or now, since he's rushing on with his question.

"I've been wondering for a loooong time, but I didn't want to offend anyone by asking," he says. "Is it true that when humans have sex, they yell 'eureka!'?"

Ooh, that's a good question. I've been wondering the same, but I've yet to meet a human I wanted to have sex with.

Percy nods slowly. "Was it a hellhound who told you that?" he asks, and we all shake our heads.

"We saw it in a YouTube clip," Dustin says. "Well, not the actual sex. It was a scene from a TV show, I think? And these guys were talking about how they shout 'eureka!' when they have sex."

"Ah. I'm sure there are some humans who do, but none of the humans I've been with have," Percy says diplomatically.

"Have you been with many?" Fabian asks. "And recently? Maybe it's a modern thing."

"I…" Percy closes his mouth. "That's a valid thought. Have you asked Noah?"

I shudder even as Fabian takes a step back in horror. "Noah, the human at CSG? He's scary."

"He really isn't," Percy assures. "But I can understand your reluctance. We'll think of another way to research this."

"I could have sex with some humans," Fabian suggests. "I've been avoiding them because they seem much more fragile than us and I didn't want to accidentally break them, but I suppose I could be careful."

"That's a great idea!" Sophie exclaims. "I will too, and then we can compare notes."

Percy leans toward me and whispers, "What's her name?"

Oops. Some host I am. I grimace apologetically.

"Before we get distracted again," I interrupt Sophie and Fabian's plan to visit the nearest town, "let me finish introducing you all to Percy."

"I'm Steffen," Steffen says, and I wonder if I should have built a tiny cottage with only one bedroom somewhere at the edge of the property. This wouldn't have happened then.

"He knows," Dustin says. "Remember? We already explained that you're not John Smith."

"Anyway," I say loudly, because Fabian has that look on his face that comes before he asks a ridiculous question, and I really don't want to hear "who's John Smith?" again. "Percy, this is Sophie, and this is Fabian."

"Didn't you know my name?" Sophie asks. "How

weird. I feel like we're old friends. I don't usually talk about sex to people who don't know my name."

"That's an excellent policy to have," Percy tells her seriously. "How many of you live here?"

"Ten permanently, including Brandt," Kethe says. "But we have people coming and going all the time."

"And I'm not always here during the week," I add. "I have to spend some time in the city handling administrative and diplomatic tasks."

"I remember what that's like," he murmurs. "At least you have this place to escape to."

Fabian smiles at him. "I like you. You're nice. I manage our records, so if there's ever anything you need to know about dragons, come find me."

"Thank you. I have a lot of questions—I know shamefully little about dragons," Percy tells him. "I may take you up on that."

Fabian puffs out his chest, beaming. He loves history and facts and compiling information, and it thrills him whenever anyone shows an interest. I have a note in my calendar to ask him a question at least once a week, just to make him happy.

"What about you?" Percy asks, looking at Sophie and Steffen. "How do you fill your days?"

"I'm in charge of Brandt's security," Steffen says, and I have to give Percy credit for not reacting beyond a polite sound of acknowledgment. Most people who find out a paranoid conspiracy theorist is in charge of security tend to freak out. When Percy's old team at CSG met Steffen for the first time, they had major concerns. But despite his tendency to catastrophize and see hidden plots everywhere, he's very good at his job.

Plus, he's a good man who needed something to fill his life.

"And I'm the Chief Health Officer," Sophie announces grandly. I raise my eyebrows.

"New title?"

She shrugs. "I'm still trying it on. I think this suits me better than just healer."

"Whatever you like best." I turn to Percy. "Sophie is responsible for overseeing the general health of all dragons. Any unusual illnesses or mass outbreaks are reported to her. She's also in charge of looking after hatchlings, dragonets, and fledglings."

"That must keep you busy," Percy says, grinning now. "I've only met one dragonet and one fledgling, but they were both a handful."

Sophie laughs. "Yes, Brandt told me about your meeting with Benisch. I went to check on him right after, and he was full of chatter about you."

"He was good company. Is he well?"

Nodding, Sophie says, "Well and in trouble again already. He's also incited his friends, and there seem to be a large number of attempted midnight flights lately."

Steffen sniffs. "I wish you'd all let me handle that."

"No," I state—not for the first time. "I'm not letting you spell fledglings in their homes after dark. What if there's an emergency?"

"There would be a key!" he protests, but I've heard this argument and I'm not having it again.

"No. They're fledglings—they're supposed to cause mischief. They'll grow out of it." I cast a glance at Dustin, who's been suspiciously quiet. He's not a fledgling anymore, hasn't been for quite a while, but until recently he still managed to cause as much trouble as one. I thought he'd finally settled down, but now he doesn't want to continue college? After he begged me to let him go?

Something's not right there.

Before I can get too caught up in planning to interrogate my grandson, Kethe interrupts. "Well, we've all had a chance to meet Percy now. Why don't you finish the tour? Lunch is in half an hour. And don't forget this afternoon."

"That's right, you said there would be entertainment this afternoon," Percy says. "What's happening?" He sounds interested and enthused, and I honestly don't think I could possibly like anyone more than I do him right now.

"We're having a reenactment!" Dustin declares, all cheerful now that we're talking about one of his favorite topics.

Percy smiles brightly. "A reenactment? Of a historic moment? That sounds amazing. I can't wait to see it."

"No," Fabian corrects. "Not of a historic moment." He turns on Dustin, his expression half accusing, half horrified. "It's not, is it? If it is, you should have consulted me! What if you got it all wrong?"

Dustin rolls his eyes. "It's not. Nobody would come to see us enact something from our history." He grins at Percy. "It's *Grease!*"

Percy blinks, then seems to get it. "*Grease*, the classic movie?"

Dustin nods.

"Ohhhh. That sounds like fun! Sorry, I got confused when you said reenactment."

Dustin and Sophie exchange glances. "Is that not right? We've been telling everyone it's a reenactment.

We've been doing reenactments every week since spring!" Sophie wails.

"Well…" Percy hesitates. "I suppose reenactment isn't exactly wrong. Usually that refers to specific people and events, though, whereas a performance of a play or movie scene, where only characters are involved, is called a… performance."

Sophie stops wringing her hands, and Dustin sighs in relief. "That's okay, then," he says. "This is definitely a reenactment. We're not playing the characters. We're playing the actors being the characters."

From the flummoxed expression on Percy's face, I guess that might not be normal.

"So… you're going to be John Travolta as Danny and Olivia Newton-John as Sandy?" he asks. "Not just Danny and Sandy, the characters?"

"That's right," Sophie says. "We're very popular. People come out from the city to see our reenactments."

"I'm sure they do," Percy murmurs. "I'm very much looking forward to this." He even sounds like he means it.

To be fair, Dustin and Sophie and their friends do an excellent job. They usually have the movie playing on a screen behind them, and sometimes you can't tell the difference between the original cast and the reenactors. And we do get lots of people out from the city and all the nearby towns to watch—not humans, of course, unless they're members of the community. I'd never let unknowing humans onto the estate.

Steffen sniffs but says nothing. We all know how he feels about letting non-dragons he hasn't personally vetted enter the grounds, but he lost that argument six months ago when Dustin pleaded for me to let some of his friends come and watch.

"Tour," Kethe reminds us. "Or you won't be finished before lunch."

"She's right," I say, taking Percy's hand and loving the tiny shiver that runs through him at the contact. "There's a lot to see." Top of the list: my rooms. The rest can wait.

CHAPTER SIX

Percy

Studying myself in the bathroom mirror, I silently chant words of encouragement. I'd do it out loud, but shifter hearing is excellent—which apparently holds true for dragon shifters—and Brandt is in the next room. The last thing I want is for him to hear me saying "I'm sexy and he wants me" to myself.

He does want me—believe me, he's made it very clear throughout the day—but this would have been a lot easier if we'd just fallen into bed right after I arrived. Sure, the waiting has heightened the anticipation, but also, the *waiting has heightened the anticipation*. What if it turns out we're not good together? I mean, the kisses we've been sneaking all day have been phenomenal, and just thinking about him makes my cock perk up, but that doesn't mean we'll be compatible in bed. What if the sex is bad? Or what if it's fine, but once is enough? I'll be faced with the awkward dilemma of either staying the night in Brandt's bed or somehow coming up with a nice excuse for leaving… at midnight… to drive two and a half hours back to the city and sneak into David and

Caolan's place. Which won't work, because David has wards to let him know when people enter, even if they're approved to do so. He'll wake up immediately and worry about why I've come back in the middle of the night, and I'll have to explain to him that it's due to bad sex. Caolan will hear, of course, and won't be able to resist telling his "bros," and… well, it'll be a catastrophe.

The pressure's on.

Brandt knocks on the door. "Percy? Are you okay?"

I draw in a deep breath. "Yes. I'm coming." I practice a seductive smile in the mirror, but it just looks like I have gas. No smile, then. I'll have to seduce him another way.

I whip off the sleep pants he found for me in the linen closet. From the way he wiggled his brows at me when he handed them over, I don't think he actually expects me to wear them, but I felt awkward about walking around naked. Plus, they help with the whole hiding-my-panties thing—the excuse of "changing for bed" gave me a reason to slip into the bathroom and tuck my underwear into a drawer until I can find a better place to hide it. Now, though, I need to utilize every weapon I have in this war of seduction. I need him to be so hot for me, he doesn't notice if the sex is bad.

Shut up. It does *too* make sense… if you don't think about it too much.

Taking another deep breath, which totally doesn't work to reduce anxiety, I turn toward the door.

And freeze.

I want this. I really do. But it's been four years since I've had sex with another person, and for decades before that, I only had sex with one person—my best friend.

There were never any nerves there. Lily and I knew nothing could make things awkward or weird between us. When you've been best friends for over four hundred years, when you know each other inside out and have been there for all the moments, big and small, there's not much that can shake your friendship. Sex is definitely not one of those things. And before that... well, I've never been much for casual sex. I'm a relationship kind of guy. By the time I got around to having sex with any of my past lovers, we'd been together for a while and intimate in other ways. I've never had sex with someone I only knew casually.

Brandt knocks again. "Percy? Please come out and talk to me. We don't have to have sex."

I groan—I'm fucking this up completely.

"Percy?" he calls again.

I grab the sleep pants, yank them back on—nearly injuring myself in the process—and open the door. Brandt is standing there, shirtless, looking all hot and concerned, and I mentally berate myself for not being able to just leap on him and enjoy what's on offer.

"Hi," he says softly.

"I'm sorry." There's so much I want to say, to explain, but those are the only words I can get out.

He shakes his head. "You have no reason to be sorry. I'm sorry that you feel you do. I never meant to put pressure—"

I laugh—well, it's supposed to be a laugh. It comes out sounding a lot more like a sob. "No, you didn't. The pressure is all coming from me. I want this; I really do. Really, *really*. You're... well, I really want this. You." Am I saying "really" too much? I make myself slow down and consider every word.

Brandt sees my hesitation and steps back. "Come and sit," he says, sweeping an arm toward the comfortable-looking sofa in front of the window. During the day, it has a glorious view over the garden and woods, but tonight it's just black outside. I follow him over and sit while he closes the drapes. Then he joins me, not sitting too close, angled to face me, and his consideration and kindness make me both want him more and feel like a loser.

"You don't need to say anything," he begins. "We can be just friends. Or we can take things slow. There's no wrong way for us to do this."

I smile. He's so lovely, and I'm so happy to have this opportunity with him. "I don't want us to be friends. I mean," I correct, "I do want us to be friends, but not just friends. I want you—a lot. I really do." *Stop with "really."* "I guess I'm just stuck in my head. It's been a while for me, and I've never had casual sex."

He jerks back. Crap, what did I say?

"Casual sex?"

Is he asking me what it means? Given the conversation we had with the others earlier today, I assumed he would know. "Uh… yeah. It's when people have sex without being in an actual romantic relationship. I mean, I know we both said we would be monogamous, but that doesn't mean a serious committed relationship. Casual sex."

"I know what it is." He waves dismissively. "I didn't realize that's what you wanted."

I open my mouth, but nothing comes out. What do I say now?

"I don't think it is." The words surprise me. "I thought it was, but talking to you this morning made me doubt it, and my little freak out in the bathroom just now proves it's not. I've… I've never had sex with someone I wasn't dating. Except Lily, and that was different." I see the question form in his gaze and hurry on. Now is not the time to talk about Lily and her death. "I've known all my… bed partners really well before we got to that stage. I thought casual sex would be fine, but it turns out it's not really for me. But I still want to have sex with you. Just not… casually."

Brandt is silent for a moment. "I want us to be friends," he begins finally. "No matter what happens, I really like you. I respect the leader you were, and I think you're an incredibly impressive man. I was sorry when you left, and not just because you're the sexiest person I've met in a long time."

He pauses, and I nod, mostly because it seems to be expected. I'm not sure where he's going with this. Has he changed his mind about wanting us to fuck?

"At no time," he continues, "did I ever think about having casual sex with you."

It's my turn to jerk back.

"Even when we'd just met and everything was chaos and politics, I was thinking that maybe in the future I'd have the chance to…" He seems to struggle for the right word. "…court you. Date you."

I don't know what to say.

"If you just want to have sex, well, I'm not going to turn you down. I'm not stupid. But that's not what I was hoping for," he finishes.

My friends were right. I'm an idiot.

"It's not?" I squeak.

He shakes his head. "I hoped you'd want to explore a relationship with me. I've been around for a long time,

Percy. I've had casual sex—a lot of it. And I've had a lot of relationships. We talked about this earlier—there's not much I haven't done. But I'm past the point in my life where I want meaningless hookups. I want a partner who'll be there for me. Don't panic," he adds. "I know that may not be you. But I'd like to see if it could be. If that's not something you want, please tell me now, and I'll adjust my expectations."

Something settles inside me. I really was fooling myself with the whole "just a fuck" thing, because hearing Brandt say these things is balm to my soul. And yes, maybe being his partner—if it works out that way—will mean constant interruptions from dragons needing his attention, countless ceremonies and events, and little time just for us. But if I'm honest, I have to admit I've missed those things.

The magic brushes against me, wrapping me in approval. I savor the feeling—it doesn't visit me much anymore, and that's another thing I've missed.

"Don't adjust your expectations," I say, looking him directly in the eye, and a smile breaks out on his face as he grabs my hands in his.

"We can go slow," he promises. "Let's just talk, and then I'll show you to a guest room. There's one with a lovely vi—"

I lunge forward and kiss him, just like I did this morning. It could fast become my favorite way to shut him up.

"That was nice," he murmurs when we finally break apart. His gaze is warm in a way that makes me hot all over.

"I don't want to go slow," I tell him. "I really don't. I don't want to sleep somewhere else." I hesitate.

"But?" he asks, and I sigh.

"I don't know you that well, and I'm worried I'll cock this up."

"How?" I expect him to sound condescending, but there's only encouragement in his voice.

"Well… what about toes?"

"What about them?" Now he sounds confused and intrigued.

"How do you feel about them? Do they gross you out? Or do you have a foot fetish? Or do toes just not factor in at all?"

He chuckles and bends forward to drop a kiss on my mouth. "I'm beginning to see why casual sex is not for you… and why you said you were stuck in your head."

I slump back into the sofa and stare at the ceiling. "I'm sorry. This will go away. I just need to know more about you so I'm not all worried about whether you're enjoying yourself. Maybe if I just ask you some questions real quick…" Way to go, Percy. Nothing's sexier than having to complete a survey before sex.

"How about you answer two questions for me?" he suggests. I roll my head to look at him. He's got that lovely sexy smile again.

"Okay?"

"Are you certain you're ready to have sex now?"

"Yes," I say firmly. "I do want this. I'm just worried I'll make it bad."

"You could never make it bad," he assures me. "But I want you to enjoy yourself too. Which leads me to my second question… Do you trust me?"

I sit up. "In what sense? I mean, I do trust that you wouldn't hurt me or anything, but I've heard enough about you dragons to know that I wouldn't trust you to plan a birthday party unsupervised."

He sniffs, a little miffed. "I'll have you know that my parties are epic. The last one had a petting zoo *and* a magician *and* a clown, and everyone came dressed as fruit."

I blink, distracted. "As… what?"

"Fruit," he repeats patiently. "I was a banana."

Right. That just reinforces my belief that dragons shouldn't plan parties unsupervised.

"But," he continues, "I meant do you trust me sexually. If I tell you to just lie on that bed and focus on me, on the sensations between us, and not think about anything at all… could you do that?"

Butterflies explode into being in my stomach, swirling wildly. A sweat breaks out along my spine.

And my cock goes rock hard.

Brandt smiles. It's not like he could miss my reaction —the dragon sense of smell isn't quite as good as a felid shifter's, but in such close proximity, the scent of arousal is impossible to miss. And these soft sleep pants do nothing to hide my erection.

But he says nothing, waiting patiently for me to make the decision. Even if I wasn't more turned on right now than I have been in a very long time, just the fact that he cares so much about my feelings would be enough for me to say yes. There's something about having someone care about me that's such a turn-on.

I shove aside the little voice telling me it's a relic from my lonely childhood and meet Brandt's gaze squarely. "Should I take off my pants first?"

His smile turns heated. "Oh, allow me." He stands, then extends a hand. I take it and let him draw me to my feet, then just… stand there as his gaze slides over me. There's something about not needing to *do* anything that's wildly arousing. My job is to let Brandt be in control, and from the amount of precum soaking the front of my cotton pants, that really does it for me.

Over four hundred years of having sex, and I never guessed I might be sexually submissive.

Brandt raises a hand and places it in the middle of my chest, right between my pecs, and I shiver. He's so warm, and his hand leaves a trail of fire behind it as he strokes down over my belly to my waistband. His fingers slide below the elastic. The pants slip a little lower on my hips. I catch my breath.

His other hand comes to help, and he eases the elastic waistband over my dick, being careful not to touch it. I can't help whimpering. I was so hoping for some contact.

The pants drop to the floor, pooling around my ankles.

Brandt takes my hands in his. "Step out of them."

I do, kicking them aside, then stand there completely naked before him. It's a little cool in here, what with dragons not needing central heat, and the chilly air kisses my bare back. The contrast with the heat radiating from Brandt in front of me and the fire building inside is… titillating.

Still holding my hands, Brandt steers me to walk backward… toward the bed, if my mental navigation is correct. The backs of my legs touch the mattress, but instead of letting me fall back, or even sit, he tugs me right up against his body.

He's in charge. Still half dressed. I'm naked, at his whim and his mercy.

My heart rate speeds up, but in a good way.

Brandt studies my face, then nods and lowers his head to kiss me again. I raise my arms to wrap around his neck, but he pulls back and shakes his head. "Did I say you could touch me?"

I nearly come on the spot.

"Sorry," I manage, dropping my arms back to my sides, and Brandt rewards me with a kiss, then steps back.

"On the bed. Lie on your back, head on the pillow."

I scramble to obey. That's all I need to do tonight: just obey. No thinking required.

Brandt sheds his own pants and climbs onto the bed to kneel beside me. His gaze sweeps over me, and I take advantage of the opportunity to look my fill at him. He has an amazing body, not overtly muscled but taut nonetheless, all long limbs and lightly furred skin. His cock is hard and straining, standing up from his lap, the ridges that prove he's definitely not from this world clearly defined. When I first heard that the elf and dragon dick had ridges, I assumed it would be more a series of bumps than anything else. I was so wrong. This is reminiscent of an old-fashioned washboard or corrugated iron. My ass twitches at the thought of how that will feel sliding in and out of me.

I can't wait.

"You seem fascinated by something," Brandt observes, and I lift my gaze to meet his.

"Oh, I am. Just thinking how much I want your cock in me."

He smiles, but his eyes darken with lust. "We're definitely going to get to that. First, I want to explore a little. You're so lovely." He strokes the fingertips of one hand down my torso from shoulder to hip, catching on a nipple along the way, and I shudder, goose bumps breaking out all over me. I reach for his hand, desperate for a firmer touch, but he tsks at me.

"Did I say you could move?"

I honestly didn't think it was possible for me to get harder, but I do, and a whimper escapes me. I need *more*.

Brandt's attention is snared by the way my dick is begging for attention, and he slides his hand from my hip to wrap around it—firmly. I groan with combined arousal and relief and suck in a breath.

"So good," I murmur.

His smile turns wicked, and he leans down and closes his mouth around my left nipple. The hot, wet heat and friction of his tongue—which is slightly rougher than I was expecting—drive me *wild*, and when he starts slowly jerking my cock in time with his laving tongue, a fog of desire takes over my brain.

Yes… yes… Brandt… yes… so close… yes…

And then he's gone.

I whine, blinking my eyes open and wondering when I even closed them. Brandt is kneeling between my legs, bent forward to examine my cock.

"What's this?" he asks, and I try to gather enough brain cells together to understand what he's talking about. "Oh, they're going away," he adds, and it clicks.

"The barbs? Uh… they only pop out when I'm about to ejaculate." I suck in a breath. "Which I'm not now."

"Patience," he murmurs, softly trailing his fingers over my balls. It's almost ticklish, but in a very sexy way. My breath hitches, and he casts an amused glance up at me. "Not enough to take you to the edge? How about this…"

He leans in a tiny bit more and captures the head of my dick in his hot mouth. Just the sight of his lips wrapped around me makes my eyes roll back.

It must have done the trick, because I'm suddenly aware of a light touch on my barbs, and I instantly come.

When my vision clears, Brandt is sitting back on his haunches and licking his lips.

"Sorry," I mutter. "Didn't get a chance to warn you."

He grins. "Don't be sorry. So, the barbs are sensitive, then?"

I can't believe he wants to talk about anatomy right now, when one part of his anatomy is prominently demanding attention.

"Yes. Very." I eye his dick. Am I still not allowed to touch him?

"I thought they'd be sharp, but they weren't."

"It's cartilage. Not meant to harm, just to… hold in place, I guess. Do we really need to talk about this now?"

He pets my cock, and it stirs to life. One benefit to being a shifter is that we have basically *no* refractory period. "I suppose there are other things we could be doing."

Yes. I start to sit up, reaching for him, but he shakes his head, and I sink back. It takes him only seconds to grab the lube from the nightstand, and then his wet finger is tracing around my hole. The muscle instinctively contracts, then relaxes, and I shiver.

This is going to be amazing. It's been so long since I've had a real cock in me.

Despite the fact that we're both panting and ready, he takes his time prepping me, until I'm begging for him to get on with it. The fact that I'm not allowed to touch him makes me so hot—all I want right now is to wrap myself around him and rub against his body.

Finally, he lines his dick up with my pucker, the pressure too light to breach me, but just enough to send pleasure impulses through my whole body.

Then he pushes inside in one long thrust.

I was right—those ridges feel incredible. Each one stretches me all over again.

Brandt plants his forearms on the mattress on each side of me, dips his head to give me a long, wet, *amazing* kiss, and then sets to work, pumping in and out of me like he's on a mission.

All I have to do is lie there and take it.

Feel it.

Every ridge catching on and forcing past my ring of muscle. Stimulating every nerve ending. Sending waves of sensation through me.

Watch his face, the way it contorts with the pleasure I'm giving him.

The orgasm overtakes me in one hard, long wave, and the last thing I'm aware of before rational thought shuts down is Brandt's shout as I clamp down on him.

BRANDT and I have sex three more times during the night. The first time, I wake to him humping slowly against my ass. The instant I make a sound, he says,

"Good, you're awake," and slides two lube-slicked fingers inside me, replaced a few moments later by his giant cock. I moan around the burn, my muscles protesting the inadequate prep, but then he adjusts to hit my prostate and everything else falls away.

The second time, he wakes me with his mouth on my balls, sucks me dry, then puts me on my hands and knees and fucks me so hard, my head collides with the headboard. I don't care. We fall asleep again with him still inside me, collapsed on top of me.

The third time, I wake to feel him hard again in my ass. He's asleep still, but we've moved at some point, rolling onto our sides. His arm is a heavy weight around my waist, holding me close, probably the reason his dick hasn't slipped out. I shift slightly, and the resulting sensations wake my cock right up. I slip my hand down to stroke it, feeling it get harder under my touch. I could jerk myself with Brandt inside me. Maybe he'll even wake up and join the party.

But it doesn't take long for me to realize that this isn't enough. I don't just want the fullness of his cock in me while I wank, I want friction. I want thrust.

"Brandt," I call softly, wiggling slightly to get his attention. His already hard dick twitches inside me, and I draw in a sharp breath.

"Mm," he mutters.

"Brandt," I say again, and he stirs.

"What?" His voice is thick with sleep, and I'm not altogether sure he's awake.

"Wake up. I want you to fuck me."

He moans a little. "Sleeping."

I huff. "Brandt, I'm horny and I want to be fucked. You're already in me—we just need some thrusting."

"You do then," he murmurs, already sinking back into sleep. I'm kind of miffed that he can sleep through this.

Fine. He doesn't want to wake up? He wants me to handle the thrusting? I can do that.

His arm really is tight around me, so I don't have a lot of room to work with, and on our sides like this doesn't give me a lot of leverage, but I'm flexible. I do yoga. I've got this.

With one hand on my own dick, wanking at a steady pace, I flex my hips, sliding a tiny bit forward and then back on Brandt's cock.

Hm. The angle's not quite right for maximum effect.

I bend my top leg, turning it out from the hip and planting my foot on the bed.

Ohhhhhhhhhhhh. Much better.

This time when I move my hips, Brandt's long, thick cock hits everything I want it to, the ridges teasing my rim and all my nerve endings. I have much more leverage this way too, so even though I can't move much, there's more force behind it. It doesn't take long before I'm breathing heavily and whimpering softly, the barbs on my cock popping out, so close, so close, so—

Brandt jerks to full consciousness behind me. "What—"

I cry out, coming so hard my vision blanks out, my ass clenching tightly around Brandt. When I can see again, I become aware of the cooling cum on my hand and Brandt panting behind me.

"You naughty thing," he murmurs, his breath hot against my neck. "Used me to get off, did you?"

"You said I could," I manage, still high on my orgasm. "Thank you."

"Well, are you going to finish the job?" he says, moving slightly and making me aware that he hasn't come yet, is still hard as a poker in my ass.

I moan. "Too tired. You do it." He starts to withdraw, but I stop him. "I mean it."

"But you're—"

"Brandt, fuck me until all I can feel is you."

A growl bursts from him, and I smile into the pillow as he slams back inside. I'm sore and tired and just came harder than I ever have before, but it's still incredibly hot to feel him pumping into me, so consumed by his lust for me that he's forgotten what a gentleman he is.

My dick is mildly interested again—damn shifter stamina—by the time he roars and convulses behind me, but I ignore it. Brandt collapses on the bed behind me, gasping for breath, his warm weight against my back so very comforting. A moment later, he slides carefully out of me.

"Who knew keeping you satisfied would be so much work?" Brandt murmurs, wrapping his arm around me again. "I can tell you're going to keep me on my toes."

I grin, my eyes closing. "Better take your vitamins."

CHAPTER SEVEN

Brandt

I WAKE FEELING loose and sated and warm all over. There's really something to be said for a night of sex. Especially with someone like Percy. He might seem all self-contained and composed, but once you strip away those inhibitions… wow.

Smiling at the memory, I turn my head toward where he should be beside me. I know he's not there, of course. My senses might not be as acute as his, but I definitely would have noticed if there was another person in the room right now. Still, the mussed sheet and dent in the pillow send a thrill through me.

Then I see the clock and leap out of bed, get caught in the damn sheet, and barely keep from concussing myself on the nightstand. How did I sleep so late?

The ache of well-used muscles as I stride to the bathroom is answer enough, and I'm smirking as I take care of my morning needs and turn on the shower. Percy isn't too far ahead of me, since there's still a trace of humidity in the air and the towel he's draped over the rail is damp. He's also neatly folded the sleep pants he only wore for five minutes last night and put them on the vanity. Remembering the wet spot that formed on the front when I propositioned him, I snatch them up. I just want a sniff before I get in the shower and wash him off me… temporarily, at least.

Something falls out of the pants and drops to the floor, and I frown. What…?

I pick it up and shake it out, but it takes my brain far longer than it should to realize what I'm holding.

Underwear. More specifically, soft, lace-trimmed, very sexy red underwear that look like they'd be cut very high…

I swallow hard.

Are these Percy's? They have to be. I picture him in them, and it's all I can do not to race naked through the house in search of him.

Deep breath. He would not appreciate that. I may not know his every thought, but I do know he's a private and reserved person, so throwing him over my shoulder and hauling him back up here while naked and waving his panties for everyone to see would not earn me any points.

Besides, the very fact that he tucked them so carefully inside the pants is a sign that he may not have wanted me to see them. I need to respect that… for now, anyway.

Sighing, I fold the pants again and lay them on the vanity, then slide Percy's delightful little secret between the layers. I'm in the shower and halfway through soaping up when I realize that if Percy's underwear are here, that means…

I moan. Somewhere in this house, my delicious little felid shifter is walking around commando. Talking to people while wearing no underwear. The fabric of his pants is sliding over his bare ass, rubbing against his cock and balls.

I've never finished a shower so fast in my life. It's only my natural grace that prevents me from slipping on the wet tile as I leap out of the stall and grab a towel.

By the time I make it down to the kitchen, where I find Percy talking to Wil and Kethe, I'm breathing heavily from my run through the hallways. This house feels a lot bigger when I'm desperate to find my honey.

"Are you okay?" Kethe asks, raising her brows at me from where she stands at the stove.

"Of course," I declare, as if it's entirely normal for me to race in like I'm being chased. "Just—er—hungry. For breakfast," I add hastily, although they probably weren't thinking I meant anything else.

Wil snickers.

Okay, so maybe they guessed that bacon isn't at the top of my priority list right now.

I look at Percy, who's sipping from a mug with a faintly amused expression on his face, and realize there's no way I can ask him to come upstairs and get naked without exposing him to a lifetime of teasing.

Sighing gustily, I slide into the seat beside him and sniff the air as Kethe brings me a plate of toast.

"Hot breakfast?" she asks, and I nod.

"Yes, please." Kethe might have only learned how to cook with Earth foodstuffs within the last few years, but she's just as talented in the kitchen now as she was back home. I begin buttering my toast as she adds eggs to the frypan. "What are you drinking?" I ask Percy. It doesn't smell like coffee.

"Tea," he replies, sipping again from the steaming cup.

I frown, because I didn't think we had any tea. Yesterday afternoon, when we raided the kitchen for a snack, he politely declined coffee, and when Kethe asked him if he preferred something else, he asked if we had any tea—the hot kind. Kethe was heartbroken to have to tell him we didn't.

So where did it come from?

I look over at Kethe, but before I can ask, Wil says, "Fabian went out last night and got some on his way back."

"And I'm so very grateful," Percy adds.

Kethe leans against the counter and picks up a cup. "I have to say, I'm enjoying it. Everyone was so excited about coffee when we got here, but this is much more soothing—much more like what I'm used to from before. And you say it comes in different varieties?"

"Many," Percy assures her. "Do you get into the city much? There's an excellent store there that imports blends from all over the world. Or I can show you a mail-order website. They have a great sample pack you could start with."

"I want some," I declare. I quickly became very fond of coffee, especially once I learned about all the different flavored syrups and creamers I could add, but this tea sounds like an experience I don't want to miss out on.

Kethe heaves a sigh, as though I'm too much trouble, then points to the cabinet where she keeps the coffee beans. I get up, bringing a piece of toast with me, and go to open the cabinet. There's a box in there I've never seen before, and inside the box are odd little packets with string attached. I pull one out.

"Is this it?" I ask doubtfully.

"Yes. That's a tea bag," Percy says patiently. "You can get loose-leaf tea, which is usually better, but not from a grocery store. Tea bags are much tidier and simpler to use, though. All you need to do is pour boiling water over it."

I take the odd little parcel to the sink, where we have a special tap installed that runs chilled, boiling, or sparkling water at the push of a button. Kethe was entranced when she saw it. I switch the mode to boiling and am about to start the flow when Percy yelps, "You need a cup! Put the bag in a cup first!"

Oh. Well, that does make sense.

As Wil and Kethe snicker, I fetch a mug and drop the *tea bag* into it, then realize how the process must work and arrange the string so it hangs over the side of the mug. It really is a rather ingenious way to avoid scalded fingers. And so simple!

Wil clearing his throat interrupts my admiration of the tea bag string, and I return to the sink and add boiling water to the mug. The water changes color immediately, and I have to admit, the fragrance that rises from the cup is rather nice.

"And now I just pull the bag out and drink it?" I ask. Percy hops up from the table and comes to peer into my mug.

"No, it needs some time to steep. Just a couple of minutes."

"You can start eating in the meantime," Kethe instructs, and I guiltily chomp down on the toast I've been holding as Percy and I return to the table.

"Have you eaten?" I ask him, and he nods.

"Yes, I had a lovely breakfast. I'm just enjoying my second cup of tea while I chat with Kethe and Wil."

"Did you know Percy grew up in England, Brandt?" Wil asks as Kethe delivers a plate of eggs and ham. My stomach growls.

"I didn't," I answer, picking up a fork. "Although maybe I should have. Your accent is different from some of the others' around here."

"Yes," Percy concedes, smiling. "It's faded a bit over the years, but it's still noticeably English, isn't it? Have you spent much time in England? There are some dragons settled there, correct?"

I nod, my mouth full of perfectly seasoned eggs. Kethe really is incredible. Fortunately, Wil answers.

"There are two groups of dragons in the UK," he says. "Neither is particularly large, though, and they're mostly independent singles and childless couples. Brandt's visited a few times, but never for very long."

I swallow and add, "The weather's odd there, too. I went in the middle of summer and it was very cold. And wet."

He nods, smiling wryly. "That happens sometimes. It's part of the reason I moved here."

"I thought you moved here because you became the lucifer," Wil says, and Percy shakes his head.

"No. CSG headquarters is wherever the lucifer happens to be living—it's moved quite a lot over the millennia. I was already living in the US when I became lucifer, so…" He shrugs. "And this is home for Sam, so he's not going to move. But who knows where the next lucifer will live?"

"I like that idea," I say, studying my tea. The color is

now quite intense. "We dragons do—did—it the same way. It's hard enough to have the life force suddenly thrust responsibility upon you without also having to uproot your life and move."

"Exactly. You can take that tea bag out now." He offers his empty cup for me to put it in, and I race to comply. I'm quite excited to taste this tea. Since I came back to Earth, there have been so many new experiences that just weren't available the last time I was here.

As I lift the mug to my mouth, he suggests, "Just have a small sip. If you're not sure about the taste, we can try adding milk or sugar—or both. Or lemon."

Ooh, that sounds fun! Obediently, I swallow only a small mouthful, savoring the liquid on my tongue before swallowing. It's very different from coffee, but Kethe is right—it's a much more familiar experience. I put the mug down and get up to fetch some cups. "I want to sample it with all the add-ins," I explain. "But I like it."

Kethe huffs and rolls her eyes, but Wil comes to help me carry the extra cups to the table and sets them out while I get the milk, sugar, and a lemon.

Percy eyes the cups. "You might need to make more tea," he suggests. I scoff.

"I only need a tiny taste. I'm a dragon. We have highly developed taste buds."

"I see." He says it solemnly, but there's a sparkle in his eyes that makes me think he's inwardly laughing. That's okay. I like his laughter.

I carefully tip a small amount of tea into each cup, then, under Percy's direction, add proportionately small amounts of milk, sugar, milk and sugar, and lemon to them.

"That tea will be cold by now," Kethe predicts when

we're done. "Especially since you've split it into little portions."

I look anxiously at Percy. "Will that affect the flavor?"

He shrugs. "Tea is always better hot, but the basic flavor should be the same. I'm sure your highly developed taste buds will manage."

He might be mocking me. I'm not sure, because he sounds completely earnest. Whatever, I'm going to do my taste test anyway.

I know right away that I don't like the tea with milk. Even with sugar added, it just tastes wrong. But I do like the one with just sugar, and the lemon is nice too.

"Could I have sugar with the lemon?" I wonder aloud, going back for another sip.

"You could add honey to the lemon," Percy suggests. "I like to have it that way when I have a sore throat."

Wil, who's been sampling each cup after me, says, "What about milk and honey? Let's try that." He looks at the table. "We need more tea."

"I don't like the milk, but we do need more tea. We need to find the perfect blend." Something Percy said to Kethe earlier pops back into my head. "Percy, did you say there are different blends of tea?"

"Yes, many. And type and flavors. This is a pretty average black tea blend. You can get unblended black teas, some excellent blends, and also green and oolong tea—and herbal teas."

Wil and I look at each other.

"A tea tasting?" he asks.

"A tea tasting!" I declare. "We must have a tea tasting. Everyone needs to be able to find the perfect tea for them. We'll call it the Tea Trials!"

"Uh," Percy says, but Kethe, who's cleaning up, agrees.

"Get some of those fruity ones like in the TV ads."

"I'll find a tea store this week and buy a big assortment," I promise. "We'll have the tasting on Saturday. Wil, you're in charge of spreading the word. Any dragon who wants to join us is welcome."

"It could be worse," Percy says to nobody in particular. "Tea never really hurt anybody."

"We should have cake to go with it," Wil suggests. "Whenever they have tea on TV, there's cake and cookies—only they're called biscuits for some reason—and little sandwiches."

"You've got a Britbox subscription, don't you?" Percy asks.

"We have *every* subscription," Kethe tells him. "And cable. There's a lot of television to catch up on."

"Is that true?" I ask Percy. "Should we have cake and cookies and little sandwiches with our tea?"

"You don't need to," he says with a sigh. "It's not a rule or anything. A good cup of tea is perfectly lovely on its own."

We wait, and he sighs again.

"But it is nice to have cake with it sometimes," he concedes.

I turn a pleading gaze on Kethe.

"Fine," she agrees. "But you better not forget the fruity tea."

"I won't, I swear." This is going to be so much fun. Maybe we should devise a points system?

I mention it, and Wil shakes his head. "The aim is to find the right tea for each person," he reminds me, "not pick a best one overall."

"Well, this has been interesting," Percy begins, standing, "but I think I'm going to need to say goodbye."

All thoughts of the Tea Trials flee my head. "You're *leaving*?" How can he just… leave?

"I hadn't planned to stay last night," he says. "I need to get back and prove to David that you didn't kidnap me for nefarious deeds. And change clothes."

My thoughts immediately go to the red panties upstairs and the fact that Percy is currently "freeballing it," as Dustin once said, and I cannot think of a single word to say.

Everyone's looking at me. Waiting for me to speak. To say something to Percy.

"Gleeeeep," I manage, and I'm extraordinarily proud of it. I clear my throat. "Do you… uh…" My gaze slips down to his crotch. If he moves, I might be able to see… something. "Uh…"

"Brandt, stop staring at Percy's cock," Kethe says exasperatedly. "He's going to think you're an animal, and we'd like him to come back."

I drag my gaze away and glare at Kethe. "I am *not* staring at Percy's cock." Think of a lie, think of a lie… "I was staring at his *zipper*."

Kethe and Wil both turn to look at Percy's crotch. Percy cups his hands over it.

"Do you mind?" he asks, but he's laughing.

"What's wrong with his zipper?" Wil asks. "Move your hands, Percy."

"What are you doing?" a voice asks from behind me, and I turn to see Fabian stumbling in. He's wearing only boxer shorts, leaving the many, many, *many* hickeys and bite marks on his torso clearly visible, and his hair is standing up on one side.

"Did you hook up with a vampire?" Wil asks, distracted from staring at Percy's pants. "Or were you role-playing being a chew toy for a hellhound?"

"I can't help it if I'm delicious," Fabian says smugly, rubbing sleep from his eyes as he stumbles over to the coffeepot. "If you must know, it was a human. The whole eureka thing is untrue, by the way. I was very disappointed." He fills a mug with coffee, leans against the counter, and sips. "What's wrong with Percy's dick?"

"Nothing!" Percy exclaims indignantly.

"His zipper, not his dick," Kethe explains, and we all turn back to look at Percy's zipper—even me. It takes me a moment to remember that it was a lie *I* told.

"Has Wil told you about the Tea Trials?" I ask hastily, hoping to distract them all.

"What Tea Trials?" Fabian asks, just as Wil says,

"When would I have had the chance?"

I wave both hands. "Explain it now. I just need a quick word with Percy." I scramble out of my seat and grab Percy's hand.

"Don't leave without saying goodbye," Kethe calls as I tow him out into the hallway.

"I won't," Percy replies, then says to me, "If you're looking for privacy, I don't think you'll get it here—not without a spell, anyway."

He's right, and it's not like I need to tell him a secret, so I stop right there in the middle of the hallway and face him. Distantly, I can hear Wil and Fabian talking, which means they're not paying attention anyway.

"How can you leave me?" I ask. It's not what I intended to say, but it slips out anyway.

He looks confused. "I'm not leaving you. I'm going back to David's place to change my clothes and check in with my friends. Won't you be back in the city tomorrow anyway?"

Well, yes, but that's a *whole day away*. And I have work to do tomorrow, so it's not like I could spend the day with him. It's going to be more than thirty whole hours before we can be properly together again.

He's clearly waiting for me to say something, so I do what any self-respecting, mature dragon wing leader would do in this situation.

I pout.

Instantly, his expression melts into a smile. "I don't want to be apart from you either," he says earnestly, blushing a little. "But it will be good for us to get some space and make sure we're still on the same page. And I'll have lunch with you tomorrow, if you're free."

Mentally, I rearrange my schedule for tomorrow and heave a big, sad sigh. "But that still leaves all of today. *And…* tonight." I deepen my voice on the last word, and Percy shivers.

"I know," he whispers. "But—"

The strident ring of his phone interrupts, and he looks a little relieved as he digs it out of his pocket. I take the chance to try and spot some… *special* movement down there, but no luck.

"It's Sam," he says, then answers. "Hey, Sam."

I hear Sam's responding shriek very clearly.

"*You went to seduce Brandt without telling any of us?*"

Percy pulls the phone away from his ear and rolls his eyes. "Sam—"

"How was it? Was it good? I bet it was good. No, don't give me details—I'm respecting your right to privacy. I am. But it was good, wasn't it? Brandt's got that look about him."

I fold my arms across my chest and smile. I always knew Sam was an intelligent and discerning man.

"Brandt can hear you," Percy says dryly, and there's a brief pause.

"Oops," Sam finally says. "Hi, Brandt."

"Hello, Sam," I say, not bothering to raise my voice. Shifters, remember? "I'm just trying to convince Percy to spend the day here and come back to the city with me tomorrow."

"Oh." Sam groans. "I am so, so, so, so very sorry, Brandt, but I need Percy back here today. I didn't know he'd left town and I told some visiting dignitaries he was here… and they'd like to see him. They leave tonight. I'm so sorry."

Disappointment stabs at me, but I understand. Ever since the life force chose me to be wing leader, my life has been in service to my people. Percy may no longer be the lucifer, but I know he's very fond of Sam and likes to support him.

"Who is it?" he asks, and Sam rattles off some names that sound familiar—I think they may have been part of the incubus/succubus delegation I met last year in Nairobi. "Oh, I'd like to see them." He looks up at me and makes an apologetic face. "I'm sorry, Brandt, but we'll definitely have lunch tomorrow."

"And you'll come and stay with me this week," I say firmly. He purses his lips, and I'm afraid he's about to say no, but then he nods.

"Okay." He finishes up his call with Sam, promising to be there in time for the formal lunch that's planned, then slips his phone back into his pocket and meets my gaze. "So…"

"So…," I echo. "I'm going to miss you."

He chuckles. "You won't have time to miss me before you see me again."

I nod firmly. "Oh yes, I will. Especially because…" I lean forward and whisper in his ear, "…I really wanted to see you wear those red panties."

He stumbles back a step, eyes wide, face flushing hotly. "Y-You saw them? Uh… um…"

"I saw. And they made me so… fucking… *hot*."

He swallows hard. "R-Really?"

"Oh yeah." I close the distance between us and lean down to kiss him but stop with my mouth just brushing his. "Promise me you'll wear them again?"

His breaths puff against my lips. "I don't wear them all the time," he says softly. "Just on special occasions and when I want t-to feel… sexy." The last word is barely audible.

I groan. "I can only imagine how sexy you are in them." Fuck, I'm getting hard. Not fun when he has to leave and it'll just be me and my hand… again.

Pressing himself against me and grinding, he whispers, "I have other pairs. Sexier ones." Then he steps back and smirks at me. "Something to look forward to. I'll text you about lunch tomorrow."

My jaw is hanging open as he saunters away, his hips swaying in a way that tells me he *knows* my eyes are on his ass.

I am one lucky dragon.

CHAPTER EIGHT

Percy

Monday morning, I stand in David and Caolan's guest room and stare at my bags as though the answer to my dilemma will just manifest.

Spoiler alert: it doesn't.

Instead, I'm just staring at a bunch of suitcases like a nutter. I heave a sigh, then turn toward the door. David's coming down the hall, and I'm almost certain it's not because he needs to use the bathroom before we leave for the office.

Sure enough, a moment later he knocks on the partly open door and then pushes it wider. "Percy?"

"I'm ready," I tell him, then cast a glance back at my suitcases. "Almost."

He looks as well, but not being as neurotic as I am, doesn't seem to see what my dilemma is.

"Did you forget something? You know you can use anything here."

I heave a sigh and shake my head. "No, I'm set. I just... Do I bring my bags? If I'm going to Brandt's tonight, the sensible thing would be to bring my bags now, right? Save the trip back to pick them up. But is that too presumptuous?"

He just looks at me for a long moment, then laughs. "Percy, you said he got all dramatic about you leaving yesterday, then he insisted you spend this week with him… how would you bringing your bags be considered presumptuous?"

I shrug, because when he says it that way, it makes me seem like an idiot. "I may have overthought it."

"Just a tad," he agrees. "Let me help."

Between the two of us, it's easy to get my suitcases down the hall to the living room, where Caolan is staring at his phone with a frown on his face.

"We're ready," David says, then asks, "What's wrong?"

"Some of these Instagram people don't appreciate you enough."

"Uh-huh. As long as you appreciate me, I'm okay with that."

"Yeah." Caolan frowns at his phone for a few more seconds, then shoves it in his pocket. "Let's go."

In the next moment, he's opened a portal right there in the living room.

"This cuts the commute right down," I tell David, who grins and gestures for me to go first. I step through the portal into the room at CSG headquarters that's been designated for this purpose. At first, the elves were just using the reception area, but that got complicated very quickly, so Sam had the wards at the office reworked to exclude this room. It means allocating security, but it's safer overall.

I move out of the way so David and Caolan can come through, then, as Caolan closes the portal, open the door into reception. This room used to house the big copier and other large-scale printing stuff, but since it's the only private room that opens directly into reception, it makes sense for it to be the portal room. The equipment got moved elsewhere.

Candice, the receptionist, looks up from her desk and squeals. "Lucifer! I mean…" She laughs. "Whoops! Percy. It's so good to see you." She comes around the desk with her hands outstretched, and I take them in mine and squeeze.

"It's good to see you too, Candice. And what's this?" I nod toward her impressive baby bump. "Congratulations!" I know Candice has been trying to conceive for about twenty years. That's actually not that long in our community, but for hopeful future parents, it feels like forever. Or so I'm told.

She beams, placing her hands on her stomach. "Thank you. We're so excited." Her gaze falls on my luggage. "Oh, are you back for good?"

"For a visit," I correct, because technically that still is all I'm committing to. "I'm between houses at the moment."

She opens her mouth to speak but is cut off by a familiar shout. Grinning, she says, "I'll leave you to it," and I brace myself and turn to meet Alistair.

"Percy, I am *very* cross with you. Why did I have to find out from someone else that you spent the weekend with Brandt having naked dragon rides?"

Behind me, Candice makes a shocked sound. There aren't too many people in reception right now, but they all turn around. I also hear the patter of footsteps from behind the security barrier, which means everyone who heard Alistair's booming voice—and there are probably a lot, since many shifters work here—has come to listen.

"There were no naked dragon rides," I say loudly, pretending I don't want to die and that my face isn't going the color of a tomato. "None."

Alistair looks both skeptical and disappointed. He opens his mouth again, but fortunately, David intervenes.

"Let's go to the office," he suggests, grabbing Alistair's arm in a white-knuckle grip.

"Ow!" Alistair exclaims, but must get the message, because he says nothing more. David half-turns to plant a kiss on Caolan's cheek.

"I'll see you later."

"Bye," Caolan says obligingly. "Al, bro, I'll text you."

David whirls. "No. There will be no texting."

Our audience stares at him.

"Just go to work," he tells his boyfriend, then drags Alistair toward the security gate. Caolan waves and heads to the elevator, presumably to go six floors down to the offices occupied by the elf king and Brandt, and I follow David, trying to act as though half the building doesn't know I spent the weekend having sex with Brandt.

David swipes us through security, and I hear the sound of people scattering back to their desks before we walk through. There are only a few standing fake-nonchalantly around as though they have nothing better to do than hover in a hallway.

"David," Alistair says, "could you loosen your grip before I lose all blood circulation in my arm? I like that arm. It's the dominant one. I'd really hate for it to fall off."

"That is the least of your concerns right now," David tells him, dragging him along.

"I don't think so. What other concerns do I have?"

"I might rip off your dick and shove it down your throat so you can't talk anymore."

"Whoa. That's very violent, David. I'm not into stuff like that. And anyway, I'm in a committed relationsh— ahh, ahh! Ouch! Okay, okay, no more talking."

I can't help smiling. I really have missed my friends.

The team office is empty when we enter, and David lets go of Alistair's arm and glowers at him.

Alistair sniffs and pouts and rubs his arm.

"Is there a reason you embarrassed Percy in front of half the office?" David demands.

"It was a genuine question!" Alistair protests. "Caolan told me that Hagen told him that Wil told him that Percy showed up asking for naked dragon rides. I just want to know why I have to find out this way." He looks at me. "I thought we were friends."

"I think I might vomit," I mutter. "How many people have heard this story?"

Alistair shrugs.

Wonderful.

"It's not that bad," David says in a misguided attempt to make things better. "I don't think many people will believe it, anyway."

That's what I'm hoping, but at the same time, hearing him say it makes me cross. "Because of the giant stick up my ass, you mean?" I snap, and Alistair actually takes a step back, his eyes wide.

"Whoa... Percy," he breathes, and I suck in a deep breath.

"Sorry," I say to David, who's... smiling?

"If you actually had a stick up your ass, you would never have said that," he tells me. "Also, I would have pulled it out and beaten you with it centuries ago. You're not your father. Get over it."

I open my mouth to say… I don't even know what, but he's still talking.

"What I meant was, not many people will believe it because they think you're reserved and shy. They don't know you're actually the kind of person who shows up at a man's house and demands a naked dragon ride."

"So it's true?" Alistair crows in delight. "Percy, I never knew you had it in you!"

I can't help laughing, though it sounds more like a huff of air than anything else. "It's partly true," I concede. "I didn't mean for anyone to actually hear that part. I was…" How do I say this without sounding insane? On the other hand, I'm talking to Alistair, so it doesn't matter. "I was trying to work out the best way to broach the subject with Brandt."

"Broach the subject?" There's an odd look on Alistair's face. "Is the subject sex? Just say 'wanna fuck?' Or lick your lips and wink." He demonstrates, and while it looks sexy on him, I'm one hundred percent sure it would look perverted and weird if I did it.

"Anyway," David breaks in, "Al, can we trust you to head off this gossip? Percy and Brandt are having a go at being together, and salacious garbage isn't going to help."

Alistair salutes. "Leave it with me. My bros and I are on the job."

David rolls his eyes. "Yeah, about that. Stop corrupting Caolan with your idiocy."

"I'm not corrupting anyone," Alistair says seriously.

"Caolan is the *master.*" He leaves before either David or I can ask what, exactly, Caolan has mastered.

I SPEND the morning in meetings. Officially, I no longer hold any position at CSG, but unofficially, former lucifers are always welcome to offer opinions, and since Sam and I actually worked together, he'd happily have me back as a full-time consultant if I wanted.

Which I don't.

I think.

No, I don't. Maybe part-time, though. It's nice to have company and use my brain for more than just reading.

The sense of anticipation grows and grows as lunchtime approaches, until I feel like I have ants in my pants. For the first time ever, I think I understand why hellhounds are the way they are: if they feel anything like this, they have no choice but to be extra.

Very extra.

Okay, no. Even with this tingling excitement rushing through me, I can't imagine doing half the things hell-hounds do. But regardless, when the clock ticks over to twelve fifteen, I decide I've waited long enough. I'm not supposed to meet Brandt until twelve thirty, but it will take a few minutes to get down to his floor. And it's not like being early is a bad thing.

I casually stand from where I'm sitting at Ellie's desk and stretch, trying to look like I have not a care in the world.

"I think I'm going to grab lunch," I say. Nothing to see here, folks.

David snorts but doesn't take his eyes off his computer screen.

"Lunch, huh?" Andrew asks, a wicked gleam in his eye. "I'll come with you."

My gut plummets. Alistair did a great job of diverting people's attention, although I think he may have given the team a full debrief, because none of them have subjected me to an inquisition—which is unusual. But my luck seems to have run out.

"No, you won't," Noah declares.

"But I'm hungry," Andrew whines. "And I haven't had one-on-one time with Percy for so long. I've known him since he was a little boy. Surely he wants to catch up with me?"

"Jesus Christ," Noah mutters.

"I'm meeting someone for lunch," I say firmly. "But we can catch up another time."

"I can't tag along?" he asks plaintively.

"No." It's said in unison by me, Noah, and David.

Andrew sighs. "You're all so mean. Fine. Why don't you have dinner at our place tonight, Percy? You can even spend the night. Your stuff is all here, after all," he adds, gesturing to my suitcases stacked neatly in the corner.

"Just go," Noah tells me. "I'll deal with him."

I don't even bother to reply, just wave as I walk out. Andrew's a good guy, solid, and one of my oldest friends, but he's a real pain in the ass.

Even with the delay and then stopping to chat for a few minutes with Candice, I'm early when the elevator doors open on the floor taken over by the elves and dragons. I'm not sure what I was expecting, but it looks just like any other corporate office reception. I approach the front desk, feeling the brush of elf magic as I walk through their wards, which are different from the sorcerer wards I'm used to.

The receptionist, an adorable twink who doesn't look old enough to vote, smiles at me. Looks are deceiving, of course—elves and dragons live as long as they want to, and they have some pretty hefty mojo for glamours and anti-aging. It's highly likely this elf is three times my age.

"Welcome," he says perkily. "How can I direct you?"

"I'm here to see Brandt," I say politely. "My name's Percy Car—"

He squeals.

Yes. Squeals.

And leaps to his feet.

"You're here! You're really here! I can't wait to tell everyone I got to meet you!"

Uh-oh. I'm guessing Alistair wasn't able to stem the gossip on this floor.

"Uh… thanks. It's nice to meet you too…?"

"I'm Dáithí. Oh, let me call Brandt—he's been so excited about you coming, he told me four times already to watch out for you."

That makes me feel better about the ants-pants feeling. I guess I'm not the only one.

Someone comes out through the security gate, and Dáithí waves frantically at them. "Tora, look, Percy's here!"

It's clearly going to be that kind of day.

As the newcomer gasps—in surprise? Joy? Fury? Who knows?—I brace myself, but someone I recognize follows her into reception and puts an end to the chaos.

Mostly.

"All right," Steffen says, scowling. "Why is Percy just standing here? Why haven't you called Brandt yet, Dáithí? What were you planning?"

"I wasn't planning anything," Dáithí says indignantly. "I was just about to call him." As if to prove it, he picks up the phone handset.

"Never mind that, I'll take it from here." Steffen's officious tone makes me want to laugh, but since he's rescuing me, I choke it back.

"Thank you," I tell Dáithí, then follow Steffen through the security gate. "I wasn't expecting such a warm welcome," I say as he directs me down a hallway, and he side-eyes me.

"Was he inappropriate? I can make him apologize. Despite what you might think, he wasn't planning to lure you into a false sense of security and then sell your organs on the black market and leave you in a bathtub."

"Oh no, I wasn't... uh, I wasn't thinking that at all. Why the bathtub?" I can't resist asking.

He shrugs. "I don't know. All the stories about organ theft mention waking up in a bathtub."

I don't know what to say to that. "Oh... well, he didn't give me an organ-thief vibe, and he wasn't inappropriate. Just enthusiastic." I can hear Brandt's voice up ahead, and just that is enough to send tingles through me—along with low-level regret that I didn't spend last night with him.

"What kind of vibe does an organ thief have?" Steffen asks. "And why would people not just avoid anyone with that vibe?"

"Do you know Alistair?" I ask. "You should really talk to him about this. It's outside my field of knowledge." Hopefully outside Alistair's too, but he does know a lot of weird facts, so maybe he'll be able to steer Steffen in the right direction.

Before Steffen can say anything else, a door opens up ahead, and Brandt's voice becomes so much clearer —and so does his scent. I breathe it in.

"…not keeping me here another second when I could be spending time with my special honey," he declares loudly to whoever else is in the room—King Raðulfr, I think, and a few others whose scents are vaguely familiar but I can't quite place. I do wince a little at being referred to as Brandt's "special honey"—though I hope he's talking about me. I'll be extremely pissed off if he's not. On the other hand, my elvish is still not great, so he could have said something else entirely.

"No one's trying to keep you here," the king says patiently. "I just reminded you to come back after lunch. Bring Percy with you. I haven't seen him in a long time."

"I'm a free spirit, Raðulfr. I'll come back if I feel like it. Maybe I'll feel like doing something else."

I turn to Steffen and raise my eyebrows. "Is Brandt okay?" He seems to be in quite a belligerent mood.

Steffen shrugs. "He doesn't like having his toys taken away."

Before I can object to that—vociferously—Brandt charges out of the room. "Percy!" he yells, and I have only seconds to brace before I'm swept into his arms.

It's nice.

Okay, it's incredible. It feels like coming home. All the ants in my pants settle, and joy rushes through me. I was such an idiot to think this thing between us could ever be purely sexual.

"You're *finally* here!" he gasps into my hair, holding me tight, and I smile.

"Having a rough morning?" I ask instead of reminding him that it's only been a day—and we talked last night and texted this morning.

"You weren't here."

Aww.

"And there was no maple syrup to have with breakfast this morning," he continues bitterly. At least I came first.

"I'm sure Kethe will restock before you go back," I soothe. "How about some lunch?"

Slowly—reluctantly—he loosens his hold on me. "Okay." He steps back and glances around. "Where are your bags? Didn't you bring them? You said you'd stay with me this week."

"They're upstairs," I explain patiently. "I didn't think I'd need them for lunch." Good thing I brought them, though.

His smile is immediate and warms me right down to my toes. "Excellent. Come on, let's go eat, and then we have an appointment."

"An appointment?" I follow him back down the hallway, ignoring the heads popping around corners to stare and the whispers that follow us. It seems that government employees love to gossip, regardless of which government they belong to.

"Yes."

"Where?"

"You'll see."

I STARE AT THE STOREFRONT. When Brandt refused all through lunch to tell me what our appointment was for, I thought it might be for something sexy. This… was not anywhere on my list of possibilities.

"Why did we need an appointment?" I ask as I follow him into the tea store. "You can just turn up and buy what you need."

"I want some expert advice," he says over his shoulder. "Choosing the right beverage is serious business, Percy. We need a balanced range for everyone to taste."

I have nothing to say in reply to that, merely a fervent hope that the proprietor will offer us a cup of tea —and possibly a good slug of whiskey to go in it. Even human alcohol will do.

Which reminds me… "Brandt," I hiss as he glances around the store. "Remember these are humans."

His expression is slightly hurt, and I momentarily feel bad for not trusting him to behave in public. He's managed to keep our secret for three years, after all. But before I can apologize, we're greeted warmly by the person approaching.

I turn and see it's the proprietor, a middle-aged human woman I know fairly well, since I shopped for tea here every week from when she opened the store fifteen years ago until I left town three years ago. Since then, it's been mail order only, and I really have missed being able to browse her selection.

I inhale deeply. It smells divine in here.

"Oh—Percy!" she exclaims. "Welcome back."

"Hello, Amara," I say warmly. "Thank you so much for keeping me stocked up these past few years."

"It's been a pleasure. And so exciting, to ship to so

many different countries. I'm only sorry you had so much trouble with the custom loose-leaf blends."

I laugh and shrug. "Not your fault." Funny story— when you send unlabeled tea leaves from one country to another, the customs department might think you're trying to import drugs. "But I will take some of that blend today, please. They never returned it after it was confiscated." A vindictive part of me really hopes they tried to smoke it instead of steeping it.

She opens her mouth to reply, but Brandt clears his throat loudly. I frown at him, surprised by the rudeness, and he says, "I'd really like to be the center of your attention at all times. Could you hold my hand or some-thing while you're talking? Just so I know I haven't been forgotten."

I choke on a laugh while my heart melts, but hold out a hand for him to take. My cheeks are somewhat warm when I turn back to Amara, who's grinning like crazy. "This is Brandt, Amara," I begin, and her grin gets even wider.

"Oh! You're the one who made an appointment. I called in one of my part-timers so you can have my full attention," she assures him. "You should have mentioned you're with Percy."

"I should have," Brandt agrees. "I'd like to tell every-body, but he can be shy sometimes."

Okay, time for me to redirect this conversation. I like Amara, but we're not *that* close.

"Did you tell Amara what you're looking for?" I prompt, and Brandt's attention is instantly diverted.

"We need a range of tea for the Tea Trials," he declares, and Amara nods slowly.

"The… Tea Trials?"

"A tasting," I explain. "Brandt's family had never tried hot tea until I introduced them to it. They'd like to try some different varieties."

"What a lovely idea," she says. "We have some great sample packs—"

"We need enough for two hundred," Brandt tells her. "Maybe more."

I blink. "Two… *hundred*?"

"Maybe more," he repeats. "Wil was in charge of invitations, and I haven't spoken to him since early this morning. But the RSVP count was at 193 then."

Who would have thought so many dragons wanted to taste tea?

"Okay," Amara says faintly. "I don't think we have enough sample packs in stock for that many people. Let's…" She looks around. "Let's start over here." She leads us toward the wall of black teas, stopping to grab two shopping baskets along the way.

An hour later, Brandt is asking his millionth question when my phone rings. I rip it out of my pocket and excuse myself, grateful for the chance of a break. I like tea, but I never wanted to know this much about it. Amara seems thrilled to have such an attentive and interested audience, but if Brandt asks one more question about damn *leaves*, I may have to take drastic measures.

I step outside the store and answer the call without even looking at the display.

"This is Percy."

"Percival? That is not how one answers a phone call."

I close my eyes. Should have looked at the display.

"Hello, Father."

"Is that all you have to say to me?"

What else does he want me to say?

"Are you well? You sound well." I wince as soon as it comes out. I basically just invited him to complain.

"Of course I'm well," he snaps, with all the arrogance of a man who believes he's above getting sick. "Not that you'd know. How do you think it looks, Percival, when my only son doesn't attend an event I host?"

Ugh... did I forget to turn up to one of his parties? No... no, I would remember if I was supposed to go somewhere. Pure fear of having to listen to him complain about it would have reminded me. Plus, there's no way I would have RSVP'd yes and subjected myself to that kind of torture.

"What event, Father? I don't recall being invited anywhere."

"I shouldn't have to invite you! You're my son. You should know you're required to attend."

Ah… this is one of *those* calls. "Of course, Father. My apologies." I tune him out as he begins his rant about duty to the family name and responsibility to heritage. The truth is, our so-called heritage is only a few generations old. When my great-great-grandmother Lisette tripped over a rock and accidentally knocked a very wealthy and influential succubus out of the way of a jealous wife's arrow, she was as common as could be. She took in washing to supplement what her husband earned as a laborer, but it still wasn't enough to properly support their three hungry children—and believe me, shifter children get *very* hungry. The succubus was so grateful to not be dead, she gifted Lisette with an estate and a big pile of riches to maintain it, then insisted all her friends welcome her "savior" into their social circle. Grandmother Lisette died when I was in my first century, but before that she told me a heap of stories, and her personal opinion is that her succubus patroness wanted her around so there would be at least one person not actively hating her guts. "A proper bitch," Grandmother called her.

Anyway, my father might like to pretend that our shit is gold, but he—and my mother—are the only ones. The rest of the family is relatively normal and understands that we just got very lucky.

I tune back in to check I'm not missing anything important. "…think it felt to have some upstart incubus telling me you were back at CSG?"

It takes me a second to put that in context. "I'm not back at CSG," I say calmly. "I'm just visiting for a little while, and Sam thought I might like to talk to Ms. Juma." I can't resist adding, "She is rather influential, you know. Was it her husband you spoke to?" The implication that Ms. Juma is too important to speak to my father directly is petty and mean-spirited, but I have to take my wins where I can get them.

Father sniffs. "Regardless, it's important you keep me informed on your movements, Percival. I don't even know exactly which misbegotten backwater you've been hiding in for the past few years!"

That's true, because I didn't tell him. I've kept our obligatory calls as short and far apart as possible and avoided any mention of where I was. It's the only way to keep him out of my business.

And speaking of my business… he's going to hear about Brandt soon. There's no way to avoid it, with the gossip already circulating so widely. I might not be the lucifer anymore, but people still know who I am, and that makes me fair game for the gossip mill.

"Well, Father, I have some news you'll be interested in," I begin. Best to preempt this—if I tell him about it now, he can't call me in a tizzy because he had to hear it from someone else. "I've started seeing someone."

He draws in a breath sharply. "Please don't tell me it's some street cleaner from whatever rural mud pile you've been visiting."

Do you see how charming my father is? Next time I think I might be turning into him, I'll remember this moment, because David is right. There aren't enough sticks in the world for me to shove up my ass to become him.

But I don't bother arguing with him—there's no point. He won't hear me, and I'll just end up frustrated and annoyed. "It's Wing Leader Brandt," I say instead, cutting to the chase.

Silence falls. All I can hear is his breathing, but I don't need him to speak for me to know what he's thinking. A dragon? But they're so *foreign*. Why couldn't I have picked someone from an Earth species? Someone with heritage and breeding, whose family could be traced back to the species wars? (Not that ours can.) On the other hand, Brandt *is* the wing leader, a position that's equal to that of our species leaders, and dragons do garner a great deal of respect... because they're dragons.

"I see," he says at last, which means he hasn't decided yet how he feels about the situation and will wait until he's thought it through to share his opinion. On the plus side, I won't have to listen to him now. On the minus, I'll get another call when he's finally ready to tell me how I've disappointed him this time. Because make no mistake, even if he decides he's thrilled with the match, he'll be disappointed with me for some reason—not telling him before anyone else, maybe, or not having introduced him to Brandt already.

Whatever it's going to be, I don't want to deal with him for a moment longer. "Father, I'm so sorry—I've been hogging your attention all this time! I know how busy you are, and I won't keep you a moment longer."

"Well, I do have many demands on my time," he admits, chuffed that I've recognized his importance. There's a part of him that's always been miffed and jealous that I, his useless and inferior son, got selected by the magic to be lucifer instead of him. That's more evidence, if we ever needed it, that the magic knows what it's doing when it selects leaders, because my father would be a terrible one.

"I'll let you get back to them, then. Thank you so much for calling. Goodbye!" I barely give him time to say goodbye back before I end the call, and then I just stand there in the cold street feeling irritated. It's a common result of talking to dear old Dad.

Finally, I put my phone away and go back into the store. Brandt and Amara have made it to the register, and Amara is ringing up the insanely large number of products they selected. They made the decision early on to only go with bagged tea, since loose leaf might be tricky to prepare for so many people—especially since those preparing it are complete amateurs. Amara takes tea preparation very seriously.

When she reads out the total somewhat hesitantly, I nearly choke. I knew Brandt was buying a lot, but... that's a *lot*. He doesn't blink, though, just hands over a credit card. CSG set the dragons and elves up with a discretionary fund when they first migrated here, wanting them to be able to establish their government and settlements comfortably without having to feel subservient or dependent on us. They integrated into the community quite quickly and have carved out a niche industry of special spells, but I didn't realize the dragons had built up quite so much money that Brandt can spend such an amount on tea.

Maybe he can't. Maybe his accountant is going to call him screaming in a few minutes.

They arrange a time for someone to collect the order—although Amara offers twice to deliver it anywhere Brandt wants for free—and then he's wrapping his arm around my shoulders and turning me back toward the door.

"Wait," I protest, wriggling out of his hold. "I need some tea."

Brandt casts a dubious glance back at the mountains of tea on the counter. "I think we have enough to share with you," he suggests.

"Are you really sure about that?" I counter, only half joking. Shifters eat a lot, but it's nothing compared to dragons. It makes sense that they'll drink a lot of tea too.

He appears to think about it, so I go back to the register and make a purchase of my own. He's *still* thinking about it when I return.

"There might be some left for you," he concedes dubiously. "Maybe of one of the kinds people don't like much."

"Good thing I got my own, then." I slide my hand into his, and his face lights up in a grin as we leave the store.

"Who was on the phone?" he asks, tugging me through the weekday throng back in the direction of the office.

Hello, mood killer. "My father. Just checking in," I add quickly. "I mentioned to him that we're seeing each other. I hope you don't mind."

His frown is immediate. "Of course I mind," he huffs, and I stop dead in the middle of the sidewalk, shocked—and hurt. "We're not *seeing* each other," he continues, then looks back over his shoulder when my hand tugs his and he realizes I've stopped. "What's wrong? Has someone hurt you?" He whips his head around fiercely, as though trying to find the mythical person who hurt me amongst the businesspeople hurrying to and from their lunch breaks and meetings.

"I'm fine," I say automatically. "Nobody hurt me." I let go of his hand and start walking again. How could I have been so stupid? Although… he did say he wanted a relationship with me. Maybe that means something different to dragons? What if this whole time, we were both talking about casual sex and this has just been a big, weird miscommunication?

Or what if the miscommunication is now, and it's my fault because I let my feelings get hurt without clarifying what he means?

I whirl around, and he runs right into me. For one brief second, I'm pressed against his broad, warm body.

Then I bounce off it and sprawl on the cold concrete. The part that bruises my ego the most? I could have saved myself, but using my shifter reflexes to stay on my feet would have been too dangerous with so many humans around. Instead, I had to tumble to the ground like a clumsy fool, and now I'm going to have bruises. Plus, I think this stupid rough concrete scuffed my favorite pants. The fabric will be ruined.

"Percy!" Brandt gasps, dropping to his knees beside me. I wince at the destruction of his pants too. Today is just not a good day for pants. "Are you okay?"

"I'm fine. Sorry, I…" Yeah, there's nothing to say. Instead, I spring to my feet, then peek around to make sure nobody noticed how easy it was. Thankfully, nobody gives a shit, except to glare at us for blocking the sidewalk.

Brandt steps up close and peers into my face. "Something's wrong," he says firmly.

"No… maybe. What do you mean, we're not seeing each other? I thought we'd decided to begin a relationship?" I can feel the heat climbing in a wave from my chest. Up my neck. Over my jaw, cheeks… all the way to my hairline. Yay. Glowing like the light outside a brothel —just what I always wanted.

"Confused" is the best way to describe Brandt's expression. "We *are* in a relationship," he says. "Is that what seeing someone means? I thought it was just dating. The precursor to a relationship."

I close my eyes. See? Miscommunication. Opening them again, I smile and lift my hand to lay against his cheek. He instantly relaxes and smiles back. "I guess it is," I admit. "Sorry. I used the wrong words."

He turns his head and kisses my hand, then takes it in his, and we begin walking again. "Words are hard sometimes. But we are definitely not in the precursor stage, in case you were wondering."

"I wasn't wondering. Just talking to my father had me off-balance, and then I misunderstood. I'm happy with what we're doing, even if some people would say we've moved fast."

He makes a pffft sound. "It's never fast between paired souls."

Only sheer will keeps me from stopping dead once more. "I beg your pardon?"

He glances over at me. "You know about paired souls. I know you do. All your friends have them."

"Yes, but… are you saying we are?" Blindly, I grope for the familiar support of the magic. It might not be mine to call anymore, but it can damn well be there for me when I need it. Its comforting touch strokes over me, and the tightness in my chest loosens. "How do you know?" I'm not an expert on paired souls, but my understanding is that only certain elves are able to see them. Not dragons.

"I asked Raðulfr this morning," he says cheerfully.

I blink. "But he hasn't seen us together since we got together." Maybe I need to ask Caolan exactly how it works. I know he's able to see paired souls.

"He doesn't need to. He's seen you and he's seen me and he's seen us together in the past. Paired souls are just people with potential to be happy forever if they choose to get together. They don't need to be already in a relationship."

"So he knew from the time he met me three years ago that you and I were paired souls?" I'm having trouble getting my head around this. "Caolan knows? Why didn't he ever tell me?"

"Did you ever tell him you were interested in pursuing a relationship with me?" Brandt counters as we reach the automatic glass doors to the building.

"That's not the point," I protest, then decide it's not

worth pursuing. But if I find out later that *David* knew all this time and didn't mention it, even suspecting that I had a thing for Brandt, I'll… well, I don't know what I'll do, but he won't like it. Maybe rip some pages out of his daily planner.

That's right. I can be vicious when I need to.

"Do you have some time this afternoon?" Brandt asks as we wait for the elevator, still holding hands. From the number of glances we're attracting, I'd guess the gossip mill is in overdrive. One sneaky young sorcerer actually snaps a picture of us with his phone.

"Really?" I ask him, and he grins and shrugs. "No social media," I insist, and he sighs.

"What am I supposed to do with it, then?"

I can't believe this is actually a conversation I'm having. "Send it to your friends. Just know that if I find out it ended up on social media, you won't like the outcome."

He grumbles but agrees, and as we get in the elevator, Brandt leans in and says—far too loudly—"I like this strict side of you. It makes me hot."

Someone else in the elevator groans. "Seriously? Do you have to do that here?"

"Shut up, Jim. It's a budding romance, and we love it and want to nurture it," someone else snaps.

I close my eyes.

Then open them real quick when a voice I recognize adds, "I love it and want to nurture it, but I'd appreciate if you could not talk about getting hot in front of me. Thanks."

Brandt winces, then glances over his shoulder. "Dustin?"

"Hey, Grandfather. I hope you enjoyed your lunch

break. In an entirely nonsexual way. No naked dragon rides, right?"

That's going to follow me into the spiritual plane and from there to my next life. I am never, ever going to live it down.

"Are naked dragon rides a thing?" the second voice, the one that so vehemently defended our right to romance, asks curiously. "Is it like a euphemism, or are there actually naked bipeds riding naked dragons?"

I am so glad I didn't look to see who the other people in the elevator are. This way, if I run into them again, I never have to know they were here to be part of this moment.

Part of me wishes this gossip would get back to my father and cause him a stroke. The other part knows he'd come back from the dead if necessary to tear me a new one over the disrepute to the family name.

Desperately, I attempt to change the subject by asking Brandt, "Did you need me this afternoon?" Then I cringe, because given the conversation was just about sex, that question is open to misinterpretation.

Fortunately, Brandt is on my side. "If you have time, there are some documents I'd like your opinion on."

"Yes. That's fine. Thank you. I'll just let someone know where I am." I don't think anyone would worry if I didn't come back from lunch with Brandt—they'd just make dirty assumptions—but it's the polite thing to do.

CHAPTER NINE

Brandt

THE MOMENT I get Percy into my city home, I toss aside his luggage and drag him to the couch.

"What are you doing? Brandt?" he asks, but from the way he's laughing, he knows exactly what I'm doing. And as lovely as that laughter is, I waste no time smothering it with kisses.

Is there anything as nice as lying on a couch with a delicious man, kissing? I want sex—we'll get to sex—but for now, just being pressed against him from head to toe, tasting him, breathing his breaths, knowing we've got all night… that's enough.

"Brandt," he murmurs, breaking the kiss long enough to nuzzle against my throat, licking along the muscles there.

"Mmm?" I ask, rolling him under me, sparing a brief thought of gratitude to Kethe's insistence that I buy the extra-deep couch.

"Nothing. I just like saying your name." He pulls back just far enough to meet my gaze and smile at me. "I love knowing it's you."

Possessiveness surges up in me. "Always me," I growl. "Only me."

He huffs a laugh and kisses me again. "Only you," he repeats. "Caveman."

"Dragon," I correct, sliding my hands under his shirt. His skin is cooler than mine, and he shivers at the contact, then snuggles even closer.

"Possessive dragon. Going to add me to your hoard?" he taunts, unbuttoning my shirt and walking his fingers down my chest.

"Maybe."

He freezes. "Wait… what?"

"What, what?" I blink impatiently. Why has he stopped?

"You have a hoard?"

There's something in his tone I can't quite decipher. Is he upset because I haven't shown it to him yet?

"Yes?"

He scrambles to sit up. "That's a real thing? You really have a hoard?"

I'm not happy with the way he's moved away from me, and neither is my cock, which was enjoying all the friction. "Of course it's a real thing."

His eyes are shiny with excitement. "That's amazing! I thought it was just a myth. What's in your hoard? Treasure?"

I am so confused right now. "Of course treasure. Why would we hoard anything we didn't treasure?"

He purses his lips, then says cautiously, "Did you have to leave some of it behind? You don't have to answer," he adds quickly.

I wince a little, because thinking of everything we had to leave behind when we came to Earth is still painful. "Yes. We could only bring those things we treasured most—and that could be transported." I make myself cheer up. "But here we get to collect new things!"

He looks sad still, so I wiggle my eyebrows and leer. "Wanna be part of my hoard? I'd dress you in… nothing. Just oils for your skin and jewels to offset your beauty. You could recline all day amongst my treasures and serve my pleasure." Hmm. That wouldn't be a proper use of him. One of the best parts of him is his brain.

Sure enough, he rolls his eyes and smiles. "Much as I love your pleasure"—he glances at my crotch—"I'd wither away from boredom."

"A challenge!" I shout, lunging for him. We tumble to the floor in a flurry of limbs and laughter, quickly overtaken by kisses.

Someone knocks on the door.

I groan.

"Brandt?" Steffen calls. "Are you okay? I heard a scuffle. If terrorists have taken you hostage, I'll find a way to rescue you!"

"Oh boy," Percy whispers.

"It's fine, Steffen. We just fell off the couch," I call. I'm pretty sure that's not going to satisfy him, but I can hope.

Sure enough, there's a pause, then he says, "Of course, fiiiiiine. I'll just go back to my place and leave you be. Nothing to worry about!"

"Fuck." I rest my forehead against Percy's. "I need to open the door before he knocks it down."

Percy laughs, but I get the door open just in time to see Steffen lean back, leg raised for a kick. "I'm fine. See?" I tell him. "Percy and I fell off the couch."

He peers over my shoulder, presumably looking for terrorists.

"Come in and look around," Percy calls, and I groan on the inside but obediently open the door wider. Will I never get to see what underwear Percy is wearing today?

Steffen marches in, eyeing the room suspiciously.

"Would you like to join us for dinner?" Percy offers, and if he wasn't so perfect, I'd hate him right now. Why is he prolonging my torture?

"No, thank you," Steffen says politely, interpreting my glare correctly. Then he opens the TV cabinet and peers in. What he thought to find, I really don't know. Toddler terrorists?

Pah! I've never met a toddler that could be quiet while hiding.

He pokes around a bit more, then nods, seemingly satisfied that all is well. "I'll leave you to it. Good night."

"Good night," Percy says. I grunt, then close the door behind him and engage all the locks and the chain. That's not to keep him out, but because I know he'll stand there until he hears me do it.

"What would you like for dinner?" Percy asks, disappearing into the kitchen, and I stare after him mournfully.

"I was hoping to have you," I call, and he laughs.

"That's dessert."

By the time Friday morning rolls around, I'm in an excellent mood. Tomorrow I get to go back to Draighaimaz and take part in the Tea Trials, which are shaping up to be an epic event. I've spent most of the week with Percy, soaking in his delightfully peaceful aura and corrupting him sexually. *And* this morning he indulged my begging and put on a very sexy pair of white satin panties with tiny red hearts embroidered along the edges. Just thinking about him wearing them all day long while we're both being responsible and businesslike makes me want to drag him into a supply closet and rip them off him right now.

But I won't.

I am a mature, responsible dragon. I can control my urges.

Anyway, he'd be *pissed* if I did. Like… I'd be sleeping alone for a while. He doesn't mind illicit workplace rendezvous—in fact, he likes them a lot—but not while he's in the middle of something. And he'd kill me if I ripped his panties. Well, not kill me, but that disappointed expression would be directed at me, and then there would be a very long lecture about respecting his property, and how destroying it reflects my lack of respect for him. He's very good—I actually cried when he lectured me about using his shirt to mop up spilled wine. Then he kissed my tears away and blew me, so it worked out okay.

But I don't want to disappoint and upset him again, not ever, so that means controlling myself until lunchtime. Especially since he's doing me a favor by even being here. We're negotiating to buy some land in the Pamir Mountains currently owned by a demon conglomerate. The land is remote enough that it would be a great place to set up a flight school for young dragons—and learning to fly in mountain air currents is always a needed skill. If you can manage the vagaries of the swiftly changing up and down drafts, you have the tools needed to fly anywhere. Talks were going well for a while, then stalled about two months ago. Percy graciously agreed to look at the documents for me this week, and this morning he sat in on a meeting with the conglomerate… and now it looks like we might actually have a deal.

I smile at the demons as we say our goodbyes and they commit to sending the final contract. As soon as Wil leads them out, I spin around and grab Percy in a giant hug.

"Thank you," I say into his neck.

"You're most welcome," he replies, chuckling and patting my back. "I didn't do much."

"It was enough. Finding a good place for a flight school has been a top priority since we got here."

Before Percy can modestly brush off my thanks again, someone clears their throat. We pull apart and glance over to the doorway. There's a very huffy-looking familiar hellhound filling the doorframe.

"Hello, Alistair," Percy says, sounding resigned.

"Alistair, get out of the way!" a voice I know says from somewhere behind him, then he jolts forward into the room, followed by Caolan.

…and Gideon?

"Good morning, Brandt," Caolan says. "Hi, Percy."

"Hi, Caolan," I reply, shooting a sideways glance at Percy, who shrugs. "Did we have a meeting?"

"Nope," he says cheerfully, popping the *p*. "Alistair and I came to find out why we haven't been invited to the Tea Trials."

Percy makes a sound that might be a choked-off laugh. "And why are you here?" he asks Gideon, who's skulking in the doorway with a scowl on his face.

"David couldn't get out of his meeting, so he sent me to make sure these idiots didn't cause an interspecies incident."

"I would never cause an interspecies incident," Caolan defends. "Brandt and I have known each other a long time."

I nod. "I don't think there's anything Caolan could do that would upset me that much," I confirm. "Maybe if he made Percy sad."

"Nobody's making me sad," Percy cuts in, using his calm voice. I have a sneaking suspicion he's trying to manage me. "Alistair, why are you sulking?"

I return my attention to the pouting hellhound. He's being a lot quieter than usual.

"You're having a party and didn't invite me," he accuses. "How could you not invite me to a party?"

"We're not having a party," Percy begins, but it's my turn to interrupt.

"Of course you're invited! I didn't know you'd want to come. We're taste-testing tea."

Alistair blinks. "What?"

"Brandt and his friends had never tried hot tea before," Percy says dryly. "Now they want to taste as many varieties as possible and pick their favorites."

"The Tea Trials!" I announce.

"Ooooh," Caolan says. "I just drink the tea David buys. I didn't know there were different kinds!"

"You're… tasting tea?" Alistair sounds confused. "I like tea. There's nothing quite as wonderful as a hot cuppa—well, except for rimming Aidan, but I'm the only one allowed to do that. But… I think you're too excited about this."

"Does that mean you don't want to come?" I ask. "I need to know if you're coming. Kethe's making cake."

"Of course we're coming," Caolan says, and Alistair nods.

"I've been waiting for a long time for someone to invite me to Draighaimaz," he says pointedly. "Although we should really talk about that name. Home of Dragons doesn't have the level of pizzazz you really need."

"What do you suggest?" I'm not at all offended by his comment. We were somewhat rushed in the naming, and I do like pizzazz. Even the word is exciting. Maybe we could call our home Pizzazz.

Alistair screws up his face in thought. "Something unusual and catchy. The more unusual it is, the less chance you'll have of the humans thinking it's real. Like… Let There Be Dragons."

"It's a place name, not an invocation," Percy points out, but Alistair just shrugs.

"Why do we have to follow traditional naming conventions? How cool would that sound in a sentence, though: this weekend, I'm going to Let There Be Dragons."

Oooh. Intriguing.

"It's too long," Caolan says, shaking his head. "If it's too long, people will just shorten it, and then it will be boring again."

Alistair points at him. "Valid point. Okay. Hmm. Dragons Are Here?"

"Why not just go with Here Be Dragons," Gideon mutters, rolling his eyes, and something clicks in my brain even as Alistair and Caolan shout "Yes!"

It's certainly not a traditional place name, but there's

something about it... I'll talk to the others who live there full-time and see what they think.

"Here Be Dragons," Alistair declares, hands up as though framing something. "It's perfect, even if Gideon did come up with it. Now, back to my original point. I've been waiting for an invitation to visit Here Be Dragons. Waiting and waiting... all these amazing reenactments I've heard about that I wasn't invited to..."

"Stop talking, Alistair," Gideon says. "You're embarrassing all of us."

"Why didn't Dustin invite you to a reenactment?" I frown. Dustin and Alistair get along quite well.

He heaves a huge sigh. "Dustin's not talking to me right now. Not since I told him to fuck his professor."

"What?" At first I think there's an echo, but then I realize I'm not the only one who said it. All of us are staring incredulously at Alistair, who shrugs.

"Apparently he's hot. Dustin was all giggly around him. It made sense."

"Is that why he's thinking of dropping out of college?" I demand. Is it because of a crush?

Alistair shakes his head. "He wants to drop out? It's been a few months since he stopped talking to me, but he was really happy then. And he didn't have any problems with this professor, so... I don't know." He frowns. "Maybe I should make him talk to me."

"Or maybe you should leave it to us," Percy tells him gently. "Let Dustin come to you when he's ready."

Percy always knows best, so I resist the urge to grab Alistair by the shirt and demand he tell me everything he knows about this professor. Dustin's more than old enough to fuck anyone he wants—and he has, according to what I've heard—but it's been a long time since he's had a crush on anyone, and I want to protect my baby grandson's feelings from being shattered. He's the only physical tie I have to my lost daughter, the only family I have left. Well, and Percy now too.

Somehow, Percy manages to calm Alistair and Caolan down and usher them out. He says something quiet to Gideon, who nods, then closes the door and comes to me.

"You're worried about him."

I nod. "He's still young. He acts all tough, but he gets crushed so easily."

He hesitates. "When you say young, you mean…?"

"He's only… wait. I need to convert it to Earth years." I squint at the ceiling and do far more counting on my fingers than I'm comfortable admitting. "A little over four thousand."

Percy coughs.

"What?"

"Nothing. Okay, so he's young. But he's old enough to manage his own life, and unfortunately, that sometimes includes getting hurt." He hesitates again.

"What?" I repeat, and he sighs.

"I don't want to overstep."

I shake my head vehemently. "You can't overstep with me. I want you to be comfortable to say anything."

He pulls a face. "In that case… I think you need to stop treating him like a child."

I open my mouth to protest, then make myself close it. I told him to say anything. Now I need to listen.

Smiling, he wraps an arm around my waist and leans against me. "He's old enough to look after himself, especially if he knows he can always come to you. That means making mistakes. If he wants to drop college, then just smile and nod and tell him the decision is his. If he needs your guidance, he can ask for it." He pauses, then adds, "That doesn't mean you shouldn't intervene if you see him doing something that could be dangerous, but this? Having a crush on a professor and not knowing what he wants to do with his life? Everyone goes through that."

I sigh as his words sink in. "You're so hot when you're sensible," I murmur. He's right. Dustin is old enough to ask for help if he needs it.

"Thank you. I don't think you give him enough credit. He was such a huge help during the migration."

I sigh. "He was such a pretty egg," I muse. "And the sweetest little hatchling. He didn't start to get troublesome until he could talk."

Percy huffs a laugh. "Do you mind if I ask about that? Dragon procreation."

"Ask away." I trap him against me, then take a few steps back and settle into a chair, cuddling him on my lap. "There, now we're all comfy. What would you like to know?"

"Well, I noticed that you… er… when we… that is, when you… orgasm, there's, uh, there's…"

"After everything we've done to each other this week, how can you still be too shy to talk about semen?" I wonder, marveling at how red his cheeks have gone.

"I'm not *shy*. There are just some things that you only talk about in the bedroom. Or bathroom. Or kitchen. Or hallway floor. Not in the office, anyway."

If I have my way, he'll be able to talk about those things everywhere we can snatch a private moment. *I wonder if that door locks?* "Of course," I agree. "You were saying?"

He glares at me. "Really? You're going to make me say it?"

I give in. "You want to know how we procreate since we don't produce semen when we come?"

His cheeks get even brighter, but he nods. "Yes. I've heard talk of eggs, but all the egg-laying species I know of still need to fertilize."

"We don't lay eggs either," I correct, shaking my head. He waits for me to continue, and if I wasn't eager for a long, lascivious lunch, I'd draw this out to torment him a little. But there's no chance I'm going to risk making him angry right now. "We're beings of energy. Our children are born of our own inner magic."

He leans back to look at me. "What?"

"When we decide to have children, we begin shedding scales. A fully mature, powerful dragon can shed a scale a day if they choose, but that's rare. Most can only manage one per week… ish. Each scale holds a certain amount of our own inner magic. The more powerful the dragon, the more magic in the scale. We gather the scales together, and when there's enough energy concentrated, they transform into an egg."

His jaw drops.

"And if couples mix their scales when they gather them, the egg is the product of both dragons—a mix of their energies."

This time, his eyes become glassy. "That's so beautiful." He sighs. "And so much easier for same-sex couples. No need for donors or surrogates."

"And for single dragons who want children," I add. "I was a single parent to my daughter." The familiar pain tightens in my chest.

"I…" Percy hesitates, and I tighten my hold on him.

"Her name was Osanna," I say. "Dustin is a lot like her. After I began to settle from my wilder years, I decided I wanted a child, so I began to shed scales. She was the prettiest red egg, all shimmery like glitter. And she was never still. Some eggs are like that—it's why we build nests for them. The last thing anyone wants is for an egg to roll away from where you put it."

"No, indeed," he says faintly.

"Well, from the moment she hatched, she was trouble. Dustin was a much calmer hatchling—I imagine he gets that from his father, who was a very sensible fellow. Osanna wasn't still from the moment she woke until she went back to sleep. And as soon as she could talk, she was asking questions." I swallow. "She was amazing."

Percy leans against my chest and slides his arms around me. "What happened to her?"

I sigh. "Éibhear and his temporal portals. When the anomalies began, the moment of her transformation to egg was one of the first that ceased to exist. She was just… gone."

"I'm so sorry."

Pressing my face against his, I breathe deeply. I've never been able to talk about Osanna to anyone but Dustin before this, but Percy is a balm for my soul. The life force stirs around us both, assuring me of what I already know—that he's mine.

"She loved Earth," I tell him. "She didn't spend too much time here, because she was still quite young when the travel ban was implemented, but she'd be thrilled to know we're safe here and that her son is able to enjoy this place."

"I'm glad. At least that can be of comfort to you. Did you lose Dustin's father the same way?"

"No." I shake my head. "He couldn't bear it when Osanna was gone. Couldn't bear living without her. We're beings of energy, and we choose the span of our lives. He chose to move on to the ether. Dustin was still a fledgling, so I had the raising of him."

Percy squeezes me. "He couldn't have been raised by a better grandfather," he says loyally, and emotion surges in me.

"Would you want to have a child with me?" I ask.

He goes still.

"Percy?"

"I… I don't shed scales." He sounds like he's making a joke, but there's a faint thread of hope in his voice that encourages me.

"It would still be our child." I furrow my brow. "Although I'm sure I remember reading something once about a hatchling born of a dragon and an Earth species." Was it a vampire? I'll need to consult with the living archive.

He swallows, then clears his throat. "Our relationship is very new, Brandt. Let's take some time to enjoy each other."

"Of course. I'm not ready to share you yet. But you're not against the idea?"

He shakes his head. "Not even a little bit."

We sit for a while, just cuddling, and it's the calmest, most comfortable, most wonderful feeling ever.

Then he stirs. "Brandt?"

"Hmm?" I press my face into his hair and breathe deep of his scent.

"If dragon eggs are formed from energy and you don't produce any semen, why do you have a penis?"

I draw back and stare at him. Is he joking, or did he actually ask such a stupid question?

He looks back at me in all seriousness.

"For sex," I tell him, my tone implying that he might be losing his marbles to not know that already.

He chuckles. "No, I get that penises are for sex. What I mean is, why are dragons equipped to have sex when they don't procreate that way?"

Ohhhhhh, I get it now. "Because it's fun. We didn't have a biped form until we met the elves and needed a way to communicate with them. That's also why we speak elvish—dragons have no spoken language of our own, you know. We never needed it to communicate in dragon form back then. When we encountered the elves and first started shifting, our bodies weren't exactly like the elves' because they wore clothes and we couldn't see all the finer details."

"This can't be real," he mutters. "Are you telling me your original biped form was like a Ken doll, with no genitals?"

"Not mine, specifically," I correct. "This was all a long time before I hatched. But yes, the original biped form for a dragon was missing sex organs. Then after a while, we noticed the elves really seemed to enjoy having sex. So we evolved sex organs to give it a try."

Silence.

"You..." He seems to be having trouble getting his thoughts together. "You... you... *evolved* so you could *try out sex?*"

"Yep." I'm actually proud of my ancestors who did that. They knew how to prioritize. "And of course once we tried it, we realized it was a must-have and kept on going."

He starts to laugh. "I'm so glad you decided sex was a must-have," he chortles. "And I'm very grateful for your penis." He pauses. "Is that why your dragon form doesn't have one?"

I leer at him. "Been looking for it, have you? Want to change 'naked dragon ride' from euphemism to reality?"

He's still laughing as he shudders. "Death by dick literally ripping me in half does not sound appealing, thanks."

"Good point." That would do terrible things for my sex life. "Yes, that's why my dragon form doesn't have one. I believe some of our people evolved them in both forms for a while, but sex as dragons isn't as much fun as sex in biped form, so it evolved away after a while."

"I didn't think evolution worked that way."

I shrug. "We dragons have always liked to do things our own way."

He smiles and leans up to kiss me. "I wouldn't have it any other way."

CHAPTER TEN

Percy

"I'M REALLY NOT sure about this," I say for maybe the thirtieth time.

"You'll love it," Brandt assures me.

Uh-huh.

"It's very safe," Wil says earnestly. "And we're doing a very ordinary launch today."

I close one eye, then open it. "What does that mean? 'Very ordinary'? What would a non-ordinary launch be?"

The three of them shrug.

"Well," Brandt says, "lately we've been throwing ourselves off the roof of the apartment building and shifting midair."

"You've *what*?" I shriek.

"We didn't have any other option," Steffen explains. "The roof of the building isn't big enough to hold even one of us in our shifted forms."

I pinch the bridge of my nose, trying not to think about what could happen if for some reason the shift didn't work or there was a strong wind or any of a million other things that would result in them plummeting fifteen stories to splat on the ground. And of course, when they died, the spell shielding them from sight would collapse, which means humans would be gifted with the sudden view of a mysteriously appearing squashed body on the street. So… yay. Gruesome deaths *and* risk of exposure to humans. A two-for-one deal.

"Why," I begin, "can you not do what we're doing right now?" I gesture around me at the high school sports field we're standing in the middle of.

They look around.

"We're only here for you," Wil says. "It's a lot of trouble to have to come here when we could just use the roof of the apartment building." My face must reflect what I'm thinking, because he hastily adds, "You're worth the effort, of course."

They seem to be missing my point, but now isn't the time to beat them over the head with it. "We'll discuss this later," I warn, and Wil and Steffen both look at Brandt, who smiles sunnily.

"I'm always happy to talk to you about anything," he assures me. "Now, do you want me to explain again?"

I eye the harness Wil's holding with a *lot* of trepidation. "I think I've got it. I still don't see why we can't take a car." A lovely heated car with upholstery and no risk of falling to my death from a great height.

My cat snarls at me in disgust. It clearly thinks I'm wimping out.

It's right.

Sighing, I take the harness and climb into it. Brandt and Wil check all the straps and buckles, then Wil, Steffen, and I stand back. Brandt disappears from sight as he raises the distortion shield, then I feel a change in air pressure and assume he's shifted.

Um…

"Did we forget to account for the fact that we can't see him now?" I ask. How are they going to strap me and my harness onto him if we can't see where we're strapping?

"Brandt," Steffen yells. "Percy can't see you."

A second later, my dragon appears before me, and I catch my breath.

"He just forgot to exclude you from the spell," Wil explains. "Come on."

Brandt turns his head to look at me as we approach, and oh my… I am not prepared to see his eyes this way. When we Earth shifters change forms, the only resemblance we might have to our biped selves is hair color—and even that can be only a loose thing. But looking at Brandt's face now, there's no way I could ever mistake him for anyone else. His eyes are the same. About a hundred times bigger, but still unmistakably his.

He's beautiful. My smile bursts from me, and I reach out and lay my hand on his nose. I'm tiny in comparison, and his scales feel nothing like what I was expecting—they're incredibly soft and supple, like leather that's been worn in perfectly. He makes a rumbling sound that… well, I have no idea what it means, but I'm getting strongly happy vibes from him, so I'll go with that.

"We can't stay here too long," Steffen warns, looking around, and for once he's not being paranoid. If someone happens to see us standing here, they might come to see what we're doing, and right now, Brandt fills most of the field, even if he is invisible. Having a human walk into him would be bad.

Wil and Steffen show me how to climb up and then get me securely harnessed to Brandt. It's weird, sitting on my boyfriend and being strapped to him. For the first time, it truly sinks in that Brandt, my boyfriend, is a *dragon*. A dragon I am going to ride. And not in the naked-fun-times sense.

Mind. Blown.

Way sooner than I'm ready for, Wil and Steffen drop back to the ground and back away. "You're clear, Brandt," Steffen calls, and suddenly Brandt's *moving*. His muscles shift beneath me, and it's all I can do to keep from shrieking as he surges to his feet. I'm so busy trying to hold in the scream that I barely notice him sweeping his wings out, and then he launches us into the air.

Blood rushes through every inch of my body. His wings beat powerfully as we climb. The lights of the city spread beneath us, and oh, wow, wow, wow… I think this might be the best way ever to commute home for the weekend.

But fuck, it's cold. Brandt's warmth seeps into my bottom half, but even with my shifter resilience to cold and my heavy coat, the top half of me is not happy about the chilly wind and temps at this altitude. Next time, I'll be better prepared.

There's a sudden rushing eddy of air, and I look right to see another dragon, a green one, flanking us. It's holding my overnight bag in its claws, which is a disconcerting sight. A quick glance left reveals a red dragon. Neither Steffen nor Wil are as big as Brandt, but they're still pretty impressive—even if I'm not sure which is which. I have time to learn these things.

I suck in a deep, lung-aching breath and grin. "Wooooooo-hooooooo!" I shout, and all three dragons make these rumbly-huffy sounds that might be laughter. Then Brandt coughs, and fire erupts from his nostrils.

Shrieking, I flatten myself to his neck as we fly through the dying flames. The warmth washes over me, but there's not enough juice in them to burn. It's actually really nice, even if all three of my companions are making those laughing noises again.

"You're a cheeky brat, Brandt!" I call, loud enough for him to hear, and he responds with another bout of flame. This time, I stay upright, confident in the knowledge that Brandt would never do anything to cause me harm. I'm flying through fire. This is the wildest thing I've ever done.

Father would never do anything like this.

I push aside the stupid little voice. Yes, my father wouldn't approve—but since I don't want to be him or anything like him, that's a good thing.

Huh. I guess I'm not turning into my father, after all.

The journey is much faster this way than by car— about twenty minutes as opposed to two and a half hours. And it's a *lot* more interesting than the highway would be. My cat loves it too, surprisingly—we've always been good with heights, but I would have thought actually flying might be different. I might have to try this one day while in felid form. I'm disappointed when Brandt slows and then circles, but disappointment quickly changes to adrenaline as we descend. Even though Brandt's velocity is just as controlled as when he launched, I can't help the feeling that he's about to lose control and we'll plummet to the ground—the ground that's rushing toward us way too quickly. The house looks lovely and warm, though, all lit up, and I cling to a wave of relief and pleasure at the thought of being home.

It's quickly followed by more alarm. I've spent one night in this house. One. Night. It should not feel like home.

As Brandt settles onto the ground and folds in his wings, I ignore all my trepidation and unfasten the straps holding me to his back. Before I can climb off, he turns his head and looks over his shoulder at me, a gleam in those huge eyes that warms me all the way through. This is exactly where I'm supposed to be. I pat his neck and lean forward to say, "I'm going to ride you so hard later."

Someone clears their throat, and I close my eyes. Seriously? Am I destined to always have someone overhear me at the worst possible moment?

Brandt makes that laughing sound, and I stomp my feet a little as I climb down. He assured me earlier that I couldn't hurt him with my "puny feet," but at least this way he's aware of my displeasure.

I jump the last few feet and land beside Dustin, who's grinning widely. "Percy, I'm really happy for you and Grandfather, but I'm starting to worry that you might have some kind of sex addiction," he teases. I shove him gently.

"Don't you start." I want to ask him about the professor Alistair mentioned, but stop myself. If he wants to share, he will. "How was your week?"

He shrugs. "Meh." Now that he's not making fun of me, he doesn't seem himself—not at all exuberant. I sling an arm around him for a hug, and he squeezes so tightly, worry surges.

Behind him, the red dragon shifts back to Wil in biped form and frowns. He raises an eyebrow and points at Dustin, and I make a face. I have no idea what's going on.

Dustin pulls back, and I school my expression into a warm, reassuring smile. The air shifts behind me, and a few moments later, I feel Brandt's presence at my back.

"Hello, beloved grandson," he says jovially, but there's a note in his voice that tells me he saw that hug and is worried.

"Hello, Grandfather. Have you been keeping Percy happy all week?" Dustin smirks. I'm relieved to see his mood lighten.

Brandt sniffs. "Of course. I've forgotten more about keeping men happy than you'll ever know."

"It's not going to do you much good if you've forgotten it," Dustin points out, then ducks under Brandt's playful swipe, laughing.

Wil and Steffen join us, and I notice that all three of my traveling companions have dropped their glamor now that they're safely home, their faces once again showing their heritage. I like it—they're all handsome even in human guise, but seeing the forms they prefer, their chosen features, is special. We begin walking up toward the house. The area designated for launching and landing is at the bottom of the garden, near the shelter of the trees and away from any buildings that could be damaged by a poorly judged descent. Apparently, my shed in Broome isn't the first structure destroyed by falling dragon. It's a nice stroll up to the back terrace, the windows glowing in welcome. We skirt the pool, which is covered for the winter, and follow the path around the side of the house to the mudroom door.

The house is gloriously warm. I hadn't realized how cold my face was until my cheeks start to defrost. We shuck our coats and troop out to the kitchen, guided by an amazing smell. Kethe looks up from the pot she's stirring.

"There you are. We'll be eating in fifteen minutes, if you want to change or anything. Percy, how was the trip? No aerobatics?"

I blink, glad nobody mentioned that possibility to me before I strapped myself to Brandt's back and let him fly me across the countryside.

"I would never do that!" Brandt declares, and we all look at him. "Not without your permission first," he adds, and I stretch up on my toes and kiss him.

"Maybe one day," I say before I can check myself, then wonder where that came from. Do I really want to ride Brandt while he does aerial cartwheels or whatever?

My cat perks up.

I guess I do. Even if the thought does make my stomach backflip.

"If you want a fun ride, I'm your best bet," Sophie says. "None of this lot can keep up with me."

Immediately, an argument breaks out over who could give me the best roller coaster experience, and I make myself a cup of tea—with one of the blends Amara sent over—and take a seat at the kitchen table, smiling as I listen to my boyfriend declare that he is too able to do a triple backflip fast enough to not lose any altitude.

And I relax.

After a raucous dinner at which Sophie insisted on describing in great detail the pus in the infected throat of a fledgling she saw this week, I leave Brandt arguing with Steffen about whether we need infrared heat sensors randomly placed around the grounds and wander into one of the downstairs parlors. Kethe has a fire going, and it's warm and cozy, the perfect place to curl up on a cold Friday night and just unwind.

"Percy?"

Or the perfect place to have a conversation with my boyfriend's grandson. From the sound of his voice, it's going to be a heavy conversation too.

I turn around. "Hi, Dustin. What's up?"

He meanders in and around the perimeter of the room, trailing his fingers over the walls and furniture. I make myself comfortable on the sofa, giving him space to work through his thoughts.

It takes a while, and I'm just wishing I'd brought a drink with me when he finally heaves a huge sigh.

"I need some advice," he declares dramatically, throwing himself down beside me.

"Of course," I reply, holding back my smile. He might be millennia older than me, but he's the sweetest kid.

"It's about college. Me quitting college, I mean."

Serious stuff. "I'll do anything I can to help," I promise.

He sighs again. "I don't know what to do. I like college… kind of. I really like this new experience, and I'm learning a lot about Earth society. Some of your science is weird, but it all makes sense in the end."

I wait.

"But I don't think I can keep going. It's tearing me apart inside."

Uh-huh. Before he continues his melodramatic monologue, I need to make sure this is what I suspect it is, and not something more serious.

"Are you being bullied, Dustin? Or harmed in any way?"

He blinks at me. "Oh no. I was being metaphorical. It's *emotional* torment."

I nod solemnly. It must be the professor crush Alistair mentioned.

"I'm in love." He says it the same way a less interesting person would say "I'm dying."

"Isn't that usually a good thing?" I venture.

He shakes his head. "Not this time. My love is unrequited. And I can't function! I can't concentrate in class, can't answer questions without stammering and saying stupid things. It's destroying me. The only solution is to drop out of college, but I really don't want to." He gazes at me tragically, eyes shimmering with unshed tears, and I'm torn between laughter and sympathy.

"Well… there might be other solutions," I begin. "Do you mind if I get a few more details?"

He lifts a hand to shield his eyes. "I'll tell you whatever I can. I need guidance… I just can't see a way out of this."

And I thought hellhounds were bad. They've got nothing on dragons.

"So… this person you have a cr——er, that you're in love with, they're in some of your classes?" I need him to tell me it's his professor.

"One. One of my classes."

"Okay, that's a good start. If it's only one class, you

shouldn't need to drop out of college entirely. Is this class only offered at one time, or could you switch to another time?" *C'mon, Dustin. Tell me it's your professor.*

He drops his hand to his lap and stares at me with big eyes. "I can't switch. Well, I could, but it wouldn't matter." He drops his voice to a whisper. "I'm in love with the professor."

"I see. That does make it more complicated," I say gravely. "Could you drop the class entirely?"

"No. It's required for my degree." He bites his lip. "Maybe I should change my major? But I really like what I'm studying."

At least he's not still fixed on dropping out as the only option.

"Well, the semester's almost over. If you can just get through a few more weeks—"

"He teaches two more of the classes I'll need to take."

Okay, there's just no winning here. "As difficult as it is being in love with someone who doesn't love you back—"

"He doesn't even know I exist," Dustin interrupts dolefully. "I'm just a name on the class list that he sometimes calls on. And then wishes he hadn't when I stumble over my words and call Shakespeare Wilbert instead of William."

I try not to wince visibly. Poor kid.

"That must be awful for you," I commiserate. "But, Dustin, college is just four years. Even if you have him for a class every year, it will be over before you know it. If you drop out or change your major just to avoid him, you're giving up something that could form a part of your life for so much longer."

He heaves another sigh. "I guess."

"That doesn't mean it's going to be easy. Maybe you could try to get out more, socialize—unrequited love sometimes fades when it's not fed. Distractions might help. Or you might meet someone new who feels the same way." The doubtful expression on his face tugs at my heartstrings. "Let me be completely honest, Dustin. I don't think dropping out is the best option. I think you'll regret it. But this is a decision only you can make, because you're the one who has to go to this class and feel these feelings."

He stares into the fire for a long time, silent. I let him sit with his thoughts and wish I could actually solve this problem for him.

"I guess it just comes down to how brave I can be," he says at last. "If only it was easier. I think I'm going to fail the class because I can't concentrate."

"That's something I might be able to help with. Shakespeare, you said?" Relief floods me. Something concrete I can do!

"Intro to English Lit," he says, and I smile.

"Piece of cake. I have a degree in literature myself. I'll help you study. Even if that doesn't make things easier, at least you can pass the class."

"Would you?" He gazes at me with a wounded, earnest expression. "That would make me feel less like a… a… failure. Loser. Idiot."

"You're none of those things," I say firmly. "You're just having a tough time with this one subject. We've all fallen in love, and most of us have had our hearts broken when that love wasn't returned. I can't help you with that, but I can help you with your classwork and take some of the stress out of the situation."

He lunges across the space between us and engulfs me in a hug. "Thank you, Percy! I feel like a weight has been lifted," he says into my shoulder. "It's not going to be easy, but finally I feel like I can actually do it."

I hug him back, patting his back gently. "It's my pleasure. I wish I could do more."

When he finally draws back, his eyes are a bit red, but he's smiling. "I'm going to go read the book for my next assignment," he says. "Thank you again. I'm so glad Grandfather found you." He leaves before I can think of a response.

I sigh and rest my head against the back of the sofa. "Are you going to come in?"

There's a faint rustle as Brandt abandons his post in the hallway and enters the salon. "Thank you for that," he says, closing the door. A moment later I feel the now-familiar wash of his power as he activates a spell—presumably a privacy one.

"There's no need to thank me. I'm just glad I could help—even if it was just by providing an ear. Did he even see you as he left?"

"No." He comes around the end of the sofa and settles beside me, taking my hand in his. "He was stuck in his own head. But he was smiling, and I'm grateful for that."

"I think he needed to talk to someone about it," I say. "Share the burden and all that."

Brandt screws up his face. "So he's in love with his professor."

I squeeze his hand. "Maybe. It's more likely just a crush, though—given he can't actually speak to the man, love seems a bit of a stretch."

He visibly relaxes. "He's not being taken advantage

of, then. I worried about that when Alistair brought it up."

"It sounded very one-sided to me," I agree. "But Dustin's old enough to make his own decisions."

Brandt looks incredulous. "You think he should get involved with his professor?"

"Not while he's being taught by him," I concede. "That's just messy. But if he were to do it—of his own free will and without undue influence of any kind—then it wouldn't be our place to interfere."

"I'm his grandfather! I raised him. It's always my place to interfere."

I say nothing, just look at him steadily, and he finally sighs.

"Which is why I would express my opinion loudly but let him do whatever he chose."

I pat his arm with my free hand. "There you go. Remember how strong he is," I remind him. "He was so great during the migration. And maybe he's struggling a bit right now, but it's completely normal. This is going to pass, and Dustin's going to wow us all. I know it."

Brandt grins, then leans in and kisses me, slowly and thoroughly. "You wow me." I don't bother to answer, focusing instead on his mouth and his warm body. It's been a long time since I've just made out with someone, long, slow kisses on a couch in front of the fire. I pull Brandt closer, swinging my legs up and sliding down under him until we're lying together, kissing and rubbing up against each other. We're both hard, but there's no rush. We have all night, and right now, this is all we need.

Brandt's lips make their way down my neck, pausing on that one ultrasensitive spot. He loves the way my whole body shudders when he kisses me there. Opening the top few buttons of my shirt, he lays kisses over my collarbone and takes a moment to lick the hollow of my throat.

"Are you still wearing those panties you put on this morning?" he murmurs, and I smile. He has a real thing for me in sexy undies and was disappointed when I told him they're for special occasions only. This morning he begged me to wear some for him and even went through my collection to pick the ones he wanted. They're sheer white satin with tiny red hearts embroidered along the edges. I think of them as my "porn virgin" panties, because the design concept might seem innocent, but the fabric and cut are definitely not.

I gave in and wore them for two reasons: I do like wearing sexy panties, and Brandt begging is not something I can resist. Especially when giving in means I'll spend the whole day imagining him taking them off me.

Which is going to happen very soon…

"Yes," I whisper. "The satin is so soft against my skin."

He freezes, then leaps off the couch and strips off in a flurry of movement. "What are you just lying there for? Get your pants off!"

I chuckle, then get up and slooooowly unbutton my shirt and slide it off. He stands there, naked and impatient, watching me. I hand him the shirt.

"Fold this, will you?"

He tosses it over his shoulder, and I choke back a laugh as I unbutton my pants, then hesitate, hands hovering over the zipper.

"Percy," Brandt growls. "I *will* rip those pants off you."

Relenting, I unzip and drop my pants, kicking them aside.

Brandt gulps, his gaze glued to my crotch. I glance down. My dick is hard and leaking precum, making the white satin transparent.

"Well?" I ask. "What do you—oof!"

Brandt tackles me back onto the couch. "You look amazing," he gasps. "The hottest fucking thing ever. I want to ride you."

Oh! We haven't done that yet. "Are you sure?"

He nods. "Hell yes." He sits up, straddling me, and traces his fingertips over the silky fabric of my panties. The touch is almost too much, and my hips buck. "Don't you dare come yet," he warns, tugging the waistband of the panties down to free my cock, which slaps up against my stomach.

"Crap—lube," I remember. There's none in here.

Brandt narrows his eyes, then holds out his hand, palm up. Does he want me to take it?

Before I can ask, a small puddle of lube appears in his palm. I stare at it.

"Dragon magic is the best," I say sincerely. He doesn't bother to respond, just gets busy stretching himself. I lie there and watch, enjoying the sight. Part of me really wants to jack myself right now, but I know the rules—and I'm glad for them. There's such amazing pleasure in giving over control and just *feeling*.

Soon enough, Brandt's wrapping and hand around my dick and positioning it, then slowly lowering himself. There's a moment of resistance, then I slide right in as he sinks down, enveloping me in tight heat.

We both moan.

"You're incredible," he whispers feverishly, rocking

slightly, then easing back up before once again sliding down.

"Let me touch you," I beg, and he nods. I need no further invitation to grab his cock and start stroking. "Lube?" I ask, since there's no precum to slick things up, and an instant later, my fingers are slippery. I set to work, jerking him off as he fucks himself on me, both of us getting hot and sweaty, our moans punctuating every movement.

"I'm going to come," I warn, and Brandt's eyes go wide.

"I can feel them—the barbs—oh fuck me!" He comes, every muscle in his body tightening as he throws his head back, and that's all it takes to drive me over the edge.

Awareness drifts back as he carefully pulls off me, then rearranges us so we're side by side, snuggled together. We lie wrapped around each other on the couch, our breathing slowly settling back to normal. I'm warm and comfy and so, so content, and my eyes slowly drift closed.

"Tell me about Lily."

And pop right back open.

"What about her?" I ask and feel Brandt shrug.

"You've mentioned her before—that the two of you were together, I mean. And I've heard a little about her. She was part of the senior team at CSG and a personal friend of yours, I believe."

I'm silent for a moment, thinking about what I want to say. "Yes. She and I were friends—best friends. We met at boarding school when we were nine."

"*Nine?*" Brandt's shock is almost a physical thing.

"Have I misunderstood? You must have still been babies."

"Almost. There weren't that many schools back then, not even for humans, so a lot of those in the community who could afford to sent their children away for school. It was that or teach us themselves. The community had a much higher rate of education, especially amongst girls, than humans did back then. It helped us to stay alive." I stare into the fire. "Of course, that didn't make it any easier on the children who suddenly found themselves far from home."

He squeezes me tight, and the memory of loneliness and fear falls away. "So you and Lily became friends?"

"Oh no. She couldn't stand me. Lily was an adventurous soul, and I'm... not. I—"

"You are," he interrupts. "You've just been conditioned not to be."

Thinking about it, he's probably right. My father had a lot of opinions about my behavior when I was a child—and now—and it was usually easier to give in than push back.

"Maybe," I concede. "But back then, I definitely did not behave adventurously. Lily thought I was boring and stodgy, and I thought she was reckless and far too noisy."

"How did you become friends?" he asks. I can hear the smile in his voice.

"Two of the much older children were picking on a group of us," I recall. "Four or five of us, including both Lily and me. There was no rhyme or reason for it, just that we were younger and happened to be in the wrong place when they felt like being vile. There was poking and shoving and calling names, and eventually, one of the other boys began to cry. I'm not sure how it happened exactly, but Lily and I looked at each other and then charged the buggers and knocked them over. It was only the element of surprise that gave us the advantage, but when the other children saw we had temporarily gained the upper hand, they joined in. We outnumbered them, so…" I shrug. "After, Lily helped me clean up a scrape I'd gotten in the scuffle and told me I wasn't a complete loss after all, and that she was taking it upon herself to make sure I turned out to be an actual person and not a boring statue. We were inseparable after that, even if she did still call me stodgy and I called her overbearing. David came to the school a few years later, and we adopted him into the group."

"I love this story. So you were friends forevermore?"

I chuckle. "I suppose. We weren't always as close after we left school. It depended a lot on what we were doing and where we were—especially back then, with communication over long distances so difficult. But we reconnected pretty regularly, and I always knew if I needed anything, she'd come—both of them would. They did," I add. "When I became lucifer, they were the first people I called. I knew I'd need a strong team of people I could trust."

Brandt says nothing, waiting, and I sigh.

"I was so lonely," I confess. "Don't misunderstand, I loved being lucifer. It felt exactly right, what I was supposed to be doing. But it's so isolating. Only with my closest friends could I be myself. With everyone else, I was always the lucifer first and Percy second… if at all. That made it impossible to connect with anyone. And I didn't want to rely only on my friends, so… I was lonely."

His arms tighten around me again. "I understand," he says quietly, and yes, he would. He's in almost exactly the same position. Dragons as a whole may be more informal than the community is, but there's still an element of distance between him and others that's not there when it's just them. Leadership has its burdens. "When did things change between you?"

My mind wanders back to that night. "I'd been lucifer for… maybe thirty years? Possibly a bit less. It had been a stupid week. I don't even remember exactly what had happened, but it was just one thing after the other, and our admin at the time, Nadege, was sick. I had a pounding headache for half the week, I remember that much. I got home on the Friday night and sat on my couch and looked around my empty home and all I wanted was someone else to be there. A hug. Someone who would take care of calling for takeout so I didn't even have to talk to another person. Just not to be alone when I most wanted comfort."

Kissing my neck, he murmurs, "Poor Percy."

I lean into the touch, feeling a bit self-conscious. "It was a big pity party. But at that moment, Lily let herself in with the key I gave her for emergencies. She had takeout and videos with her, and she seemed like the fulfillment of all my dreams." I snort. "Not really. Neither of us ever thought things between us were more than just friendship and sex. But it meant so much to not be alone anymore."

"That's normal. I'm so glad she was able to give that to you—and I'm sure you gave her just as much in return."

"I hope so." Tears prick my eyes. I really do hope Lily got everything she needed from me. She was such an amazing friend, and having her love and support made a huge difference to my life and mental health. I would maybe have turned out like my father if she hadn't so often threatened to beat me with the stick supposedly lodged in my ass. "I miss her so much. She would have been so thrilled to meet you—all of you, I mean. Dragons and elves." I hesitate, then add, "But you specifically. I think she would have really liked you for me."

"Because I'm so charming and handsome?" he teases, and I laugh.

"Of course. And fun. She always wanted me to meet someone fun. It used to drive her nuts when I'd date someone reserved. She said I needed a partner who'd keep me from fossilizing."

It's his turn to chuckle. "You'd be the sexiest fossil ever. I'd be thrilled to brush off your dust. Oooh, maybe we can play archeologist and fossil, and I'll reveal you bit by bit."

I choke, I'm laughing so hard, and when I try to sit up, I fall off the couch.

Lily was right. I needed someone fun.

CHAPTER ELEVEN

Percy

"…THINK THAT WOULD BE A GOOD IDEA?"

I smile at my new friend Alke as I slowly rock her hatchling. Knowing what I do now about how difficult it is for dragons to have children, that they sometimes have to wait decades or even centuries for enough energy to build, I am so, so honored that she's given me her baby to hold… and that she's asking my advice.

Confused, but honored.

"I think it's a wonderful idea. Maura is going to grow up amongst all these other species, so there's no reason why they can't be her playmates from the very beginning." Maura is one of only three hatchlings in the dragon community. There are a few fledglings and quite a few older children of various ages, but mostly the surviving dragons are adults. As they become more comfortable and settled, the birth rate should increase— not many dragons were willing to procreate while their world was literally coming to an end—but it's early days yet. Alke is concerned about Maura not having any playmates to grow up with and wanted to know if I thought she should join some Community of Species parent groups.

"There are some elf children nearby," she says, "and of course I'm more comfortable with them—no offense." I smile to show her none was taken. "But I don't want Maura getting to school age and only then meeting other species. And I think it's important that she sees me making friends with other species too." She worries her lower lip with her teeth.

"You've obviously thought this through very carefully, and I can tell what a wonderful, considerate mother you are. Of course it's difficult to meet new people for the first time, especially when you're from different cultures, but I promise you, parenthood is universal."

She laughs. "You're so easy to talk to. I'm sure you have better things to do than listen to me fret while you rock Maura." Her warm gaze lands on her daughter in my arms.

"Not at all," I assure her. "I already know which teas I like best," I add dryly, tipping my head in the direction of the many trestle tables set up on the lawn with trays of shot glasses, hot water urns, tea bags, and teapots. There are approximately two hundred and fifty people —mostly dragons, but some others—wandering around with scorecards in hand, tasting the various teas and then noting whether they like them or not. It's astonishingly organized, especially for something pulled together in a week, but I still can't quite wrap my head around how excited everyone is.

Those of us who aren't tasting—or are taking a break—are settled on the terrace with the outdoor heaters. I'm in a very comfortable deck chair, and there's a small table beside me that keeps getting refilled with cups of hot tea and plates of cake. Every time someone comes to talk to me, they bring me an offering of food. It's delightful.

And I've had a lot of people come to talk to me. The word has got around that Brandt and I are together, and it seems like everyone wants to meet me. A lot of them also ask for advice, specifically about problems they're having settling into the community. I know King Raðulfr and CSG set up an outreach program for people to call with stuff like this, but I guess the dragons, at least, feel more comfortable with someone Brandt has, er, vetted personally. So to speak.

Impulsively, I suggest, "Why don't we host a parents' group here one weekend? Not just for babies, but kids of all ages. It will give you and anyone else who wants to the chance to interact and make new friends without having to go in cold."

Alke's face lights up. "Oh, would you? I'd feel so much better meeting people with you and Brandt around."

"Let me talk to Brandt and Kethe," I say, wondering if I've overstepped but also knowing that once they hear this story, they'll be all over arranging it. "I'm sure it will be fine." I smile down at Maura. "She's going to be part of the uniting generation, after all."

"The uniting generation. I like that. It's… Sometimes it's hard to think about what we had to leave behind, but knowing she's going to grow up safe makes everything worth it."

I don't say anything, just reach over and pat her hand. I need to talk to Brandt about the counseling service he and King Raðulfr set up. It seems to me that a lot of people who need it aren't using it.

Maura stirs a little, and I stroke her soft cheek. She's only just started shifting to biped form in the last few weeks and still prefers to be in dragon form most of the time. Her scales are the softest thing I've ever felt in my life, and she's such a pale pink, she's almost white. I've been told that means she'll be a red dragon when she reaches maturity.

That's something new I learned today—a dragon's color deepens as they grow older. That's why Brandt is such a beautiful iridescent shade while some of the others are a little plainer. They haven't lived long enough to get that shimmer.

Maura opens her big eyes and blinks at me. "Is she likely to fuss?" I murmur, still rocking her gently. "I don't want to upset her."

"I don't know," Alke admits. "She hasn't spent much time with strangers. Let me take her—we've had enough of your time, anyway."

I carefully hand her over, giving her one last cuddle, then make sure Brandt has Alke's number and promise someone will call her with the arrangements for the parents' day. She's only ten feet away when someone else slides into the chair she just left.

It's David, cradling a cup of tea—a full cup, not one of the tasting shot glasses. I glance around. "You didn't bring me one?"

He snorts. "I figured you've had enough. This is the first chance I've had to get near you all afternoon."

I snag a small square of lemon pound cake from the plate beside me and take a bite. "Yes, everyone's feeling quite chatty today."

He says nothing, so I look up to find him staring at me.

"What? Do I have crumbs?" I pat my mouth self-consciously.

"No, I'm just wondering if you genuinely think people are being chatty." He raises a brow.

"David, I love you, but I am not telling you and those hooligans who used to work for me that you were right. It's just not going to happen." Even if they were right. Damn them.

He laughs. "Okay, I won't hold my breath waiting. But it's nice to see you with people to look after again—and they clearly respond well to you."

I look back over the lawn and purse my lips. "About that… don't you think it's weird? Brandt and I have been together for a week, most of these people don't know me, and yet they're all acting like I've always been the one to ask advice of."

"You're forgetting about the magic," he reminds me. "These last few years have taught me that dragons, especially, are more attuned to it than we are. They rely on it and their intuition a lot. Plus, Brandt has been their wing leader for thousands of years, and they trust him. If he's brought you here, they know that means something."

"I suppose." I have noticed this week that the dragons are very intuitive. I thought shifters relied on instincts a lot, but dragons take that to the next level.

"It's not like you're some rando from the street," he adds dryly. "You were the lucifer for five decades, Percy. You made the decision to invite these people to live here, thus saving their lives. Why shouldn't they trust you?"

I don't say anything for a moment, then sigh. "I really like this."

"This, as in…" He waves at the lawn and the milling dragons and the inexplicable argument that's broken out over whether sugar or honey is a better sweetener for tea. Brandt hastened over to mediate but seems to be getting drawn into the debate. I love that he takes so much pleasure from small things, that he's delighted by simple parts of life.

"Yes. The chaos, the people treating me like family, and everyone wanting my opinion."

He studies me. "Why are you saying it like it's a bad thing?"

I shrug. "Shouldn't I be striking out and establishing myself as… I don't know, anything except a government official-type person. I should be… establishing a career. Or something."

"Oh, hello, Mr. Caraway," David says. "Forgive me for not recognizing you sooner. I wasn't expecting to hear your words from Percy's mouth."

I grab a paper napkin from the table and throw it at him. "Shut up."

"No, seriously, if you're just going to parrot your father's views and opinions, why were you concerned about turning into him?"

"I'm not parroting his views and opinions," I protest, although really… I kind of am. "But surely I should be doing something with my life? Not just falling into old habits."

"You *are* doing something," he says with forced patience. "Percy, I want you to consider something."

"What's that?" I can't help feeling somewhat suspicious. He's going to say something that makes me feel stupid. I just know it.

"Maybe you're doing what you're supposed to be doing. You're a nurturer. Maybe your purpose in life is to look after others and give them guidance. Maybe these aren't old habits but actually the 'career you should be establishing.'" He makes air quotes, and I want to hate him for mocking me, but I can't.

I open my mouth to reply—with what, I'm still not sure—but he waves me to silence. "You wanted some time away after your term was up, and I thought that was a good idea. You deserved a break. But let's face it, Percy, if you had a driving vocation for some other career, you would have felt it by now. You're not an infant. You have a handful of degrees under your belt, and you'd worked in a dozen different industries before you became lucifer. The fact is, some of those jobs you enjoyed, but you never loved them. You were good at them, because it's not in you to work at something you can't do well, but they were always just jobs."

I can't argue with that, so I keep quiet.

"Did you ever feel like being lucifer was a job?"

The words hit squarely, but I protest anyway. "That's not a fair judgment. The magic selected me to be lucifer. It would never have done that if I couldn't make—" I shut my mouth. I'm just proving his point.

He smirks. "Exactly. Leadership and nurturing are your calling. *And* you get the bonus of a loving relationship. With naked dragon rides."

I wince. "That's going to haunt me for the rest of my life."

"Probably," he agrees. "But that's not the point."

"It's not the point," I concede. I've been letting my father's opinions drive me even while I tried to stay away from him. Yes, he thinks I should be in a prestigious, high-earning career that he can boast to his friends about. The only reason he approved of me being lucifer was because it was a job nobody else could have—essentially the most prestigious job in existence, selected by the magic alone. He definitely would not approve of me being a part-time government consultant and full-time spouse to Brandt. But, as I remind myself so frequently, I am not my father. We don't think the same. For me, this past week has been the best since I left CSG, and that's not even counting the sex.

Being Brandt's partner and supporting his dragons is what I want to spend my life doing.

A weight lifts off my chest.

"Oh!" The surprise in my voice is very clear, and David smiles.

"Accepting your fate makes a big difference, huh?"

As if he knows what we're talking about, Brandt turns and waves, a big smile on his face. I wave back. This is where I'm meant to be.

David clears his throat. "Uh, not to ruin this moment or anything, but you should know that your father isn't happy."

I sigh. "When is he ever happy?" I ask rhetorically. "If you mean about me and Brandt, I know. I spoke to him at the beginning of the week. I think he'll come to terms with it."

"Well, I heard these rumors yesterday, and he's fuming. He may have heard about the whole naked dragon ride thing and feel like the fami—"

"—family reputation has taken a knock." I sigh again. I've been hearing that my whole life, and I'm so sick of it. I don't want to have to live up to his idea of what the family reputation should be. I just want to live my best life.

"Just be ready," David cautions. "He's probably going to call and yell. Have, uh, have you spoken to Brandt about him?"

"No," I mutter. And if I have my way, I'll be able to put it off for a long time. Telling my supportive boyfriend that my father is a pompous old windbag tyrant is not high on my list of fun things to do.

"It might be a good idea. Just so he can't be blindsided."

The thought of my father blindsiding Brandt is not a good one. Not until I imagine what Brandt's response would be—that lifts my spirits somewhat.

"Thanks," I tell David. "For everything." I'm not just talking about this conversation. When I was suddenly invested as lucifer, David was the first person I called. I knew I'd need someone to help me through it and have my back, and there's no one better for that than a combat sorcerer with a deep-seated need to organize every minute of the day. It was he who brought Gideon and Elinor and then Sam into the team. He kept my secret when Lily and I were hooking up, and he comforted me when we lost her. My time as lucifer— hell, most of my childhood—would have been very different without him.

"No thanks needed," he says. "I'm just glad this is happening for you." Then he chuckles. "I think it's time for me to move along. I'm getting the evil eye from those people casually standing over there."

I glance over and notice that there are four dragons hovering about fifteen feet away, sneaking looks in our direction. The next wave of advice seekers. I smile at them, then tell David, "Go away."

"I'm going, I'm going." He stands. "Will we see you at the office next week?"

"Yes." I'm not willing to be apart from Brandt for a whole week just yet, even if this place does feel like home. Besides, I can visit with dragons just as well there as here.

CHAPTER TWELVE

Brandt

THE DOOR to my office bursts open, and Steffen leans in. "Quick!"

I'm on my feet and halfway to the door before he finishes speaking. He may be paranoid, but he rarely uses this degree of urgency. "What's wrong?"

Caolan is in the hallway with him. "David called and said you need to go up to Percy immediately."

I start to run. They keep pace with me, and I barely notice all the startled faces on the people ducking out of our way. "What did he say, exactly?" I demand as we burst into the reception area. A quick glance at the numbers above the elevator has me heading for the stairs.

"Just that Percy needed you."

I start out taking the stairs two at a time but have to slow after a while. My flight stamina may be awesome, but it doesn't help much for running up stairs.

We finally make it and crash through the door into the reception area. Candice, the sweet young pregnant demon who rules the front desk, gasps, but Elinor, who used to work for Percy, is waiting for us.

"This way," she orders. "They're in the office."

"Who is?" I ask, trying not to snap. Percy only came up to visit with his friends for a while. Nobody at CSG would say anything to upset him—Sam wouldn't allow it.

"His father," Elinor spits, then sucks in a deep breath. "David's furious. Sam's holding him back."

"What happened?" Caolan gasps in shock. I understand. The idea of level-headed David needing to be held back…

"I don't know, exactly. His father turned up and demanded to see him. Candice asked him to wait while she checked, and he got snippy with her. She was almost in tears when she called through. Percy was in with Sam, so I went to walk Mr. Caraway back while David went to get Percy. He said not one word to me, the rude twat. Percy and Sam were both in the office when we got back, and Mr. Caraway started in right away about Percy not living up to his potential and casting shame on the family heritage. That's when David called Caolan, and as soon as Mr. Caraway heard him say your name, Brandt, he went on a rant about Percy prostituting himself and being subservient and all kinds of other shit that makes even less sense. David threw a sorcery weave at him, Mr. Caraway shifted, and Sam had to step in and keep them apart."

Oh no. My poor Percy. He's going to be so mortified. Especially when I walk in and eviscerate his father for upsetting him.

I can hear raised voices up ahead—well, one raised

voice—and assume that's my target. I pick up speed—only to have Caolan grab my arm.

"Have faith in Percy," he hisses, and I stop dead.

"What?"

"He's the man who ripped out the throat of his enemy as calmly as if he was checking the time," he reminds me. "He might need your support right now, but he doesn't need you to fight his battles."

He's right. A shout from the office ahead distracts me for a moment, but I turn my attention back to Caolan. "What do you know?"

He hesitates. "Not much. But David has said some things about Percy's father. Percy needs to handle this. If he needs you, you'll know."

I let that sink in as I cover the last stretch of corridor and enter the office. It's a standoff: Sam is in the center, arms outstretched in "keep back" posture toward David on one side, who's actually being physically held back by a widely grinning Noah, and a man who must be Percy's father on the other side. Percy has the same hair and eye color, but the resemblance stops there. My Percy doesn't have that nasty sneer or cold energy. My Percy is welcoming warmth and calm—even now, when he's stressed out of his mind.

He's standing near Sam, facing his father, who's ranting about dignity and how Percy hasn't got any. David makes a sound, Noah tightens his grip, Sam growls, and Percy sighs.

He looks over at us in the doorway. "Caolan, could you take David out of here, please? Before he does something irreversible to my father, who doesn't seem to realize how much danger he's in right now."

"I'm not leaving while this cretin is here," David

snaps, easily breaking free of Noah's hold and taking a threatening step forward.

"So help me fuck, David, if you don't stop right now, I will make you regret it for all eternity," Sam threatens, then he spins his head and glares at Percy's father. "There had better not be one more nasty word about Percy from you. He is loved here, and I won't tolerate it!"

Percy's mean little turd of a sire opens his mouth to say something, but Percy speaks first.

"Father, you're making a scene."

His mouth closes. His eyes narrow, and he sniffs.

"I don't know why we need an audience, Percival."

"Percival," Noah mouths. I'm with him. It doesn't suit Percy at all.

"We wouldn't have one, Father, if you hadn't come storming in here like a child."

Whoa. A delighted grin crosses my face. "You are so sexy right now," I blurt.

His father's face goes tomato red. "This! This is how you blemish our heritage," he blusters. "People are talking about my son going for naked dragon rides, and this… this… person is casually demeaning our family heritage in an office!"

"Hey!" I snap. "Percy is more than just his family, and I would never demean him!"

"This is not to be borne, Percival," he continues, ignoring me. "People are talking. About you. And this…" He sneers at me. "This *dragon*."

"That's not actually an insult," Noah says helpfully. Everyone ignores him.

"Father—"

"You have a duty to your family to maintain our

heritage in a manner that does us proud," the—what did Elinor call him? Twat?—twat rambles on. Percy's shoulders hunch, and my dragon roars within me.

"Sam, would it cause an interspecies incident if I threw this *twat* out that window?" I ask.

Sam, who looks angrier than I've ever seen him, shakes his head. "I'll take personal responsibility for it," he assures me, and Percy's father gapes at him.

"You're the *lucifer!*"

Sam shrugs. "*Mr.* Caraway, Percy has been my friend and mentor for years. I don't appreciate this disruption to our day or your stupid lecture. Percy's perfect."

I really like Sam. I should invite him out to the estate for Kethe to feed.

The twat sniffs. "I don't dispute that at all. Percival is a Caraway, and as such has the lineage"—Noah groans—"and upbringing of a true gentleman. Perfection is expected."

"I really hate you," David says.

"However, Percival's behavior of late clearly reflects that of the company he keeps. Especially this..." He glares at me. "...*dragon.*"

"Still not an insult," Noah mutters. "Can we throw him out yet?"

I glance over at Percy, who's staring at the floor. This needs to end.

"Percival, you're obviously at loose ends since your term as lucifer ended. You've allowed yourself to be swayed by the wrong crowd into abandoning your responsibilities. This scene today is a result of your behavior, and I'm certain you regret it. I'm here to take you home. We'll find you a respectable position and a suitable companion."

It takes a moment for his meaning to become clear, and then I lunge at him.

"Motherfucker!" Elinor shouts as she, Caolan, and Steffen grab me. I don't want to hurt them, so they'd better fucking let go so I can *kill that bastard.*

"Brandt, stop!" Percy's voice is sharper than I've ever heard it, and I freeze in shock. "Father, you're correct. This scene today is my fault."

"No!" I snap as David shouts, "It's not!"

Percy holds up a hand and slices me a sideways look that's both chilling and reassuring. "It's my fault," he repeats, "because I've never pushed back on this absurd belief of yours that I will fall into line with your expectations."

"Percival—"

"No, Father, I'm talking now. You had your turn. I've always been hesitant to begin an argument with you. We're family; I do love you, oddly enough, and I never wanted to cause strife within the family. But that's done now. You cannot come here and insult my friends and loved ones. You cannot. I won't allow it. The company I keep is warm and loving and supportive, and that's why I don't ever come home, Father. Because I certainly never got any loving support from you."

"Percival—"

"It's still my turn to talk. The magic selected me to be lucifer, and then when my time was done, it selected Sam. We both surround ourselves with the same people. You should take that as an indication of the type of company the magic finds important, Father. In plain words, it's not you." He takes a deep breath as his father's jaw drops. "I will not accept any criticism of my friends, and I certainly won't accept a single negative word about Brandt. He makes me stronger and more confident than I've ever been. I love him and will be spending my life with him and his dragons, and if you can't embrace that and show civil regard, then I will happily consider myself disowned and will publicly attest to that."

My dragon roars again, but this time with joy and pride. I stop straining, and Steffen exhales in relief.

The twat begins to sputter. "Disowned? Publicly? There's no need for that. If you'd just come home and live up to your potential, Percival—"

"What the fuck?" a voice snaps behind me, and I glance over my shoulder to see Gideon and Andrew in the doorway. "Sam, are you okay?"

Sam rolls his eyes. "I'm fine." He glances at Percy. "But I think Percy's dad has outstayed his welcome."

Percy nods. "Father, when you're willing to accept my terms, you can call me. I don't want to hear from you until then."

"Can I throw him out, Percy?" Andrew asks. "I've been wanting to throw him somewhere since the first time we met." He smiles wide, showing fangs. Since vampires control the descent of their fangs, it's a deliberate intimidation tactic. I stifle the urge to remind everyone I called dibs on throwing the twat out. I really do like Percy's friends. They should all come out to the estate for a visit. We'll have a barbeque or something.

"Father, the choice is yours. Leave of your own accord, or Andrew escorts you out."

"And me," David says grimly, something sparking around his hands. "I get to escort you out too."

The twat sniffs. "I'm leaving. When you are ready to apologize, I will receive you and help you claim the life you wer—"

"For fuck's sake, dude, take a hint and leave," Noah advises, letting go of David, who begins to pace steadily forward. The twat takes the hint and flees toward the door, where we all graciously part for him to go. Andrew and Gideon follow him out.

I look over at Percy. More than anything, I want to go to him and take him in my arms, whirl him around and laugh for the sheer joy of knowing he loves me, but this moment is his. And it may not be a happy one for him.

"Percy," David begins, then falls silent when Percy raises a hand again.

"Thank you for defending me. I'm sorry you had to do that. Thank you especially for throwing that weave at him—an itchy rash, wasn't it?"

David nods. "It feels like a slap on impact, so most people don't realize the worst is yet to come. He'll be very uncomfortable tomorrow." He pulls a face. "I didn't think you'd appreciate it if I used anything else."

Percy smiles. "No, I don't want him dismembered. Just a little less focused on my life." He glances around. "Thank you all. I'm so sorry you were subjected to this, but I appreciate your support."

"Anything for you," Sam says, and it's supported by nods from everyone else. "I'm just sorry I couldn't let David take him down."

"If it happens again, just let nature takes its course," Percy advises with a wink, making everyone laugh. "Now, I hope you'll all excuse me. I need a word with Brandt."

"Of course," Sam says. "Maybe head home after that? We can finish our discussion next week or whenever."

I'm barely listening at this point, too keyed up at the thought of finally getting some private time with Percy to make sure he's okay and talk about what he said and tell him I feel the same way. As he comes toward me, I wave a hand in casual farewell to everyone and turn to the door, only to stop when Steffen catches hold of Percy's sleeve.

"Do I need to worry? Is he likely to retaliate? What resources does he have?"

Is he fucking kidding me? Can't he tell Percy and I need to go home and declare our love to each other in passionate, flowery poetry, followed by energetic, sweaty sex for the rest of the day? And maybe tomorrow.

I look at my beautiful Percy and the way he's patiently listening to Steffen and telling him no, the twat is not going to mount a full-scale assault on the estate, and change my mind. Definitely tomorrow too.

"Steffen, you and Wil need to cancel all my appointments for the rest of the day and tomorrow. And Percy and I might not make it back to the estate this weekend," I add.

Steffen and Percy turn to stare at me, but Noah sniggers, and Caolan claps his hands and whips out his phone. "You're sweeping him off his feet!" he exclaims, busily typing away. Percy swipes the phone out of his hands, ignoring his indignant yelp, then half turns and tosses it to David.

"Give me a half-hour head start," he orders, and David nods, grinning. "Steffen, there's nothing to worry about. My father has a lot less influence than he thinks.

The worst he can do is bluster and gossip, and he won't do that for fear of damaging the family name. Relax."

Steffen doesn't look convinced, but he nods.

"Great." Percy grabs my arm and tows me the last few steps to the door. "I need a word with Brandt, but we'll be back in a bit."

"Really?" I ask plaintively. "We could take the rest of the day off. And *talk*."

"We don't need the rest of the day," he says briskly, pulling me down the hallway toward reception. We pass Andrew and Gideon on their way back, and Percy pauses only long enough to ask, "Is he gone?"

"We put him in a cab," Andrew confirms. "Are you—"

"I don't have time to talk right now, but I'll come and find you in a bit," my suddenly bossy lover says. Andrew seems surprised, but then a wicked grin crosses his face.

"Okay. Have fun!"

Percy goes bright red but continues dragging me along. Behind us, Andrew laughs, a dirty-sounding *heh heh heh*.

"I'm going to regret that later," Percy mutters as we enter reception. "Go press the button for the elevator," he orders, and I obey. This domineering side of him is very sexy.

He crosses to Candice's desk, and I hear him apologize for his father's rudeness, which just infuriates me all over again. How *dare* that twat-man come here and cause Percy embarrassment? I'm still fuming when he rejoins me and slips his hand into mine.

"Stop thinking about it," he commands. "We have other things to focus on."

I agree, but I'm not sure we're talking about the same things. Love and sex should not make him sound like he's preparing for war.

The elevator dings, and the doors slide open. It's empty, and Percy hustles us in and hits the door close button, then the button for the ground floor, then, to my astonishment, once the elevator begins moving, he hits the emergency stop button. The elevator slams to a halt —between floors, from the looks of it.

"What—?"

He drops to his knees and reaches for my belt. "You have one job. Keep the technician busy."

I blink at him. Is this really happening? Is my shy, reserved Percy really going to—

"Good afternoon, can you hear me?" a voice says through the speaker in the panel, and I jump. Percy takes advantage of my distraction to open my pants and pull out my half-hard cock.

"Uh, yes, I mean, no, what was that?" I stammer, suddenly realizing what Percy meant. I really hope there's no override for the emergency stop. How does it even work, anyway?

"Sir, can you hear me?"

"You're breaking up," I lie, my dick reaching full, throbbing erection as the sensation of Percy's hands pairs with awareness of the situation. Percy smiles at me, then closes his mouth around the tip.

My head falls back against the wall with a *thunk*.

"What about now, sir? Can you hear me now?"

"Uhhhhh…"

"Sir, are you okay? Do you need medical attention?"

Fuck. Must. Think.

"Sir?"

"Hey, uh, hi. I can only hear every, uhhhh"—fuck, Percy, *yes*—"every, uh, third word."

"Do you need medical attention? I repeat, do you need medical attention?"

He sucks me deep, and I lose about half my brain cells.

"Sir? Do you need medical attention?"

Distract the technician. "Uh, medical assistance, did you say?"

"Yes. Do you need medical attention?"

"No, I'm fiiiiiiiiiiine." The groan takes over.

"Sir?" the voice is beginning to sound suspicious. "Sir, why did you press the stop button?"

"Say again? I missed… that." Percy does that swirly thing with his tongue that always makes my eyes roll back, and it's all I can do to hold in my gasp. I'm not going to last long, even with this nosy technician dividing my attention.

"Why did you press the stop button?"

Looking up at me, Percy sets to work in earnest. "Ahhhh. I'm… ahh-ah-ahhhh. I'm meditating."

There's a momentary silence from the speaker, and I take advantage of the reprieve to clench my teeth and screw my eyes shut. I really want to draw this out, experience every second of the pleasure Percy can give me, but we don't have time. He might be indulging in risky behavior, but it's only because he trusts me to ensure he won't be caught and publicly embarrassed.

Knowing he has that faith in me—and the steady suction he's introduced—is all it takes to send me over the edge, and I clamp my jaw tight to keep from making a sound.

"You're meditating?" the voice says skeptically as Percy releases me and I suck in air through my nose.

"Yes," I croak.

"In the elevator?"

"Yes." This time, it's more of a gasp. Percy tucks me into my underwear while I lean bonelessly against the elevator wall.

"Why are you meditating in the elevator, sir?"

"It…" I suck in a breath. "It was the only quiet place I could find."

"I see. Are you nearly finished, do you think?"

I gaze at Percy as he climbs to his feet, grinning widely. There's an unmistakable bulge in his pants, and I reach for it.

"Not quite. I need a bit longer."

"Sir," the technician begins as Percy steps back, shaking his head, "if you're not having an emergency, you can't stop the elevator."

I raise a brow at Percy, but he shakes his head again and mouths, "Later." I pout, because I was quite looking forward to making him come in an elevator, but give in.

"Okay. I'm done, then." I refasten my belt, the only thing Percy left undone.

The tech hesitates. "You… are?"

"Well, I'm not getting much mindful awareness done with you yammering at me, am I?"

Percy slaps a hand over his mouth, eyes dancing with laughter.

"So sorry to have interrupted your mindfulness, sir," the tech says dryly. "If you're sure you're finished, and you definitely don't need any medical or other assistance, could you please press the emergency stop button again?"

Percy obediently leans over and presses it. The elevator shudders in a not-appealing way, making me very conscious of being suspended in a metal box, where I couldn't possibly shift to save myself from falling to my death, and then begins to glide downward.

"Have you pressed it? Are you moving again?" the technician asks.

"Yes. Thanks for your assistance and have a nice day!" I declare.

There's another pause. "Uh, you too. Whatever." Then a click, and the voice is gone.

I grab Percy and haul him in for a kiss. He tastes like my beautiful Percy and adrenaline and the sheer joy of doing something reckless.

"I love you," I gasp between kisses, and he draws back, making me whine with impatience. "Perrrrr-cy…"

"Are you just saying that because I said it before?" he demands. "You don't have to say it, Brandt."

Yanking him to me again, I steal another kiss before telling him, "I'm saying it because I love you. I love every part of you, even the ones you haven't shown me yet. It made me so incredibly happy when you said it, but that's not why I'm saying it now."

He lets out a shaky breath and leans his forehead on my shoulder. "I couldn't let him talk about you like that. Not you, the one person who makes me feel like I can do anything."

"You *can* do anything," I say fiercely. "You *did*. You told him to leave. You took control of your life. You blew me in an elevator."

The laugh that bursts from him sounds almost like a sob, but when he lifts his head, he's smiling. "I did, didn't I? I wanted to do something to prove I can be my own person. And I wanted you. The two matched up quite nicely."

Before I can reply, the elevator slows and stops, the doors sliding open with a *ding* to reveal the busy lobby of the building. There's nobody waiting.

"Are you sure I can't tempt you to sneak off home for the afternoon? You, me, a big bed, lots of time to explore properly…" I wiggle my brows suggestively, and he laughs again, this one sounding much more normal.

"As wonderful as that sounds, we need to go back up so I can sort out this mess and get on with our life," he says firmly, pushing the button for the CSG floor. "I've been very good at pretending my father doesn't exist, that his expectations didn't exist, and look where it's got me. This time, I'm facing the issue head-on."

"You're so sexy when you're bossy," I muse. "Wanna boss me around later?" I expect him to laugh again, but instead he smirks.

"Sure."

My dick goes hard faster than it ever has before.

CHAPTER THIRTEEN

Percy

As my brain swims toward consciousness, I'm aware of how amazing I feel. It's not just that I'm warm. That the bed is comfortable. That I spent last night in the sexual marathon to end all marathons and currently feel boneless.

It's mental peace.

Brandt loves me. I love him. I love his dragons, and I'm excited to be his helpmate as he guides and leads them. I love this house that feels more like home after just two weeks than any other place I've lived in my entire life. I love knowing that the people here like and respect me and want me here. And finally, finally, I love that I told my father to back off. No longer is there the niggling awareness that he'll call soon and I'll need to fob him off. Or worse, the fear that I might give in to him and end up as a banker or some other career I'm completely unsuited for while dating a man chosen for his pedigree and wealth rather than the fact he adores me and makes me laugh.

Instead, there's just peace. I'm warm. I'm wrapped

in the arms of a man who loves me. What more could I ask for?

"Peeeeeeeeeeerrrrrcccccyyyyyyyy!"

Clearly I should have asked for a lazy Saturday morning.

Brandt bolts upright behind me as someone pounds on the bedroom door. The thing about privacy spells is that they're one-way only, so whoever is outside can't hear us, but we can hear them very clearly.

"Percy! Percy! Percy!"

And whoever it is—Dustin? Fabian?—seems to really want to speak to me.

"I'll kill him," Brandt declares, climbing over me in his haste to get to the door and commit murder. I grab his ankle as it flies past, and he jerks back and falls to the floor. "Umph!"

Seizing my advantage, I grab my robe and put it on while walking to the door, where I can hear both Dustin *and* Fabian calling me as they hammer away. Flipping the lock—which we started using after Wil strolled in last weekend while we were fucking—I open the door.

"Good morning."

"Percy!" Fabian shouts. "I need your help!"

"What's wrong?" I ask, not sure if I should be concerned. Fabian can be somewhat dramatic, even for a dragon.

"My problem is more urgent," Dustin declares. "Really urgent. Help me!" His eyes are wild.

"I'm going to give you both an urgent problem to worry about," Brandt snaps from behind me.

Dustin and Fabian glance over my shoulder, then simultaneously step back. I try not to laugh.

"It can wait," Fabian says. "I'll see you at breakfast." He turns and flees down the hallway.

Dustin stands his ground. "I'm sorry, Grandfather, but I really need Percy's help."

Brandt growls, but when I glance over my shoulder, he's walking toward the bathroom.

"Come in," I say to Dustin, gesturing toward the couch by the window. He walks over, then hesitates.

"Is it safe to sit? I mean… have you and Grandfather—"

"Please don't finish that sentence," I beg. I might be embracing my new wild side, but it's not really that wild. Wild lite. And wild lite doesn't need to have a conversation with Dustin about the things I do with his grandfather who raised him. "It's safe." Kind of.

He collapses dramatically onto the couch, then immediately sits up and leans forward. "Look at this!"

I take the phone being brandished at me and look at the screen. It's gone dark, so I wake it up and am met with the lock screen.

I hand it back. "Unlock."

He heaves a dramatic sigh, lets the facial recognition do its thing, then passes it over again.

There's an email open on the screen, and I skim over it. Is this supposed to be bad? Good? "Uh… is this what you wanted me to see?" Maybe it's the wrong email? "It's a reminder that you have an assignment due in a few weeks?"

"Exactly!" he exclaims.

Uh-huh.

"Are you not ready? Did you forget about it?" I remember what it's like at college—I've been several times. It's easy to hyperfocus on one subject and let another slip through the cracks. "I could help you, if you like?" The course is English lit, which is something I'm rather good at. After all, I read many of those books when they were newly released.

"*No*, Percy, you're not paying attention!"

Oh-kay. I look back at the email, trying to see what I'm missing, and then it clicks. English lit. "This says you need to meet with your professor to get some feedback on the thesis," I say slowly. Oh dear.

"Yes!" He falls back against the couch, his face a study in tragedy.

"And this is the professor who—"

"Yes," he hisses, peering toward the bathroom door to make sure Brandt doesn't hear. It's still closed, and I can hear the shower running, so he's safe.

I think about the best way to respond. "Would you like sympathy or a solution?"

Dustin huffs. "Sympathy first. Solution later. If there even is one for this horrible situation."

Biting my lip to keep from laughing, I clear my throat. "It's not fair that you're in this position. Life sucks so hard."

He nods gloomily. "It does. What am I going to dooooooooo?" he whines, and in this moment, he reminds me a lot of Brandt when he's being dramatic.

"You poor thing. Could there be anything more difficult than this?" I'm so proud that I actually manage to sound sympathetic. And I *am*, to a point—after all, crushes are hard. But it's not the catastrophe he's making it out to be.

"I don't know," he mutters. "I guess maybe. But not

by much." Heaving a huge sigh, he looks over at me. "I guess I'm ready for a solution now."

I grimace. "I don't have much to offer," I apologize. "Unfortunately, you have to meet with him. Unless… is his TA taking any of the meetings?"

He shakes his head. "No. This is the one stupid professor who wants to do them all himself." He pouts, looking almost on the verge of tears, and my heart aches for him.

"So you'll have to meet with him, then. But it probably won't be too long a meeting." I glance back at the email, which includes a short summary of the assignment and the purpose of the meeting. "This says you need to pitch your thesis to him and give a brief overview of the direction you're taking with it. You can rehearse all of that beforehand, get so used to talking about it that it's automatic."

He sits up. "Maybe then I won't freeze and stammer and say dumb things." There's a note of hope in his voice.

I nod. "I can help you. You prepare what you're going to say, and you can practice with me. I'll ask you questions and everything. By the time you need to go to the meeting, you'll be so familiar with what you need to discuss that you'll be able to say it without thinking." I sound a lot more confident about this than I actually feel. The power of the crush is infinite, and it's entirely likely that Dustin will still blush and stutter when faced with his "hunky professor."

Dustin jumps up from the couch and grabs me in a hug. "You're the *best*, Percy. Thank you!" He gives me a smacking kiss on the cheek, then heads toward the door.

"I'm going to start work right now. The sooner I know it inside out, the better." And he's gone before I can reply.

The sound of slow clapping draws my attention to the bathroom door, where Brandt is leaning in the doorframe, towel wrapped around his waist but not hiding his erection, water droplets slowly rolling over his chest. I nearly swallow my tongue.

"You're truly wonderful with my family," he says.

"Mmm," I agree, only partly paying attention. There's this one bead of water that's about to hit the towel…

"It makes me so happy to see them rely on you… although I wish it wasn't when we're in bed."

"Right," I say absently. If he gets just a little bit harder, that towel will fall, I'm sure of it.

He chuckles and straightens, and I enjoy the way his muscles flex. "My eyes are up here, Percy."

Dragging my gaze away from his abs, I look at his face. "And they're very pretty, but what makes you think I'm with you for your eyes?"

Laughing outright, a bold, joyful sound that makes me smile, he steps forward and very deliberately drops the towel. "What is it you're with me for, then?"

A shriek from the hallway interrupts me, and I realize with a wince that Dustin didn't close the door when he left.

"My eyes!" Sophie shrieks. "My eyes! I need to pluck them from my head! And brain bleach! I need brain bleach to wipe this image away!"

Forget Here Be Dragons, we should call this place Drama Central.

LATER IN THE DAY, Brandt and I sneak off for a walk in the woods. It's been a while since I've had the chance to enjoy nature like this, so I shift and let my cat have the reins for a while. Brandt is thrilled by that and spends a full fifteen minutes stroking my fur, rubbing my face, and crooning "Who's a pretty kitty? You are. You're my pretty kitty." My cat loves the attention, soaking it up as his due, but the rest of me is cringing at the thought of having to eventually shift back and look him in the eye after I rolled onto my back for a belly rub.

Although… last night he rimmed me, so what's a little belly rubbing after that?

Eventually we get started on our stroll through the trees, Brandt chatting idly about the security measures in place and the ones he had to talk Steffen out of. I agree that infrared sensors in the woods would have been overkill—not to mention annoying, what with all the wildlife around here. It's a really pretty estate, and it backs onto national park, so there's plenty of room for frolicking, even for creatures as big as dragons. They just need to be careful about people being close enough to see them.

We've crossed off the estate by the time Brandt suggests a break, and I curl up beside him when he sits on the damp ground at the crest of a hill. The view here is lovely, and my cat rumbles contentedly—even more so when Brandt begins to stroke my head.

"Are you happy here?" he asks quietly. "I know what you said to your father yesterday, but… it's a big commitment, taking on me and my baggage."

I shift back to my biped form and cuddle up against his side. "I know. If you'd asked me six months ago—

hell, even two months ago—I would have said I didn't want this kind of responsibility again." He tenses, and I grab his hand. "But I would have been so wrong. I was so focused on discovering myself that I ignored the fact that I know exactly who I am. My time as lucifer was the most rewarding period of my life. It was a job I loved with every fiber of my being, even on the days I hated it. When it was over, I thought that part of my life had to be over. I was an idiot," I admit. "I knew I didn't want to be what my father wanted from me, and I couldn't be lucifer anymore, so I went traveling in hopes of discovering my passion."

"And you didn't find anything?" His tone is careful. I shake my head.

"No, because it was right here all along. My friends said it: I like nurturing people. Looking after them. Helping them solve problems. It's why the magic chose me to be lucifer, to guide the community—and why my time ended when they needed something different. Your baggage isn't baggage for me. And even if it was… I love you enough to deal with that."

He kisses the top of my head. "I won't be wing leader forever," he says. "It's been a long time already, and I think I have a while longer ahead of me, but eventually the life force will select someone else to take over."

"And we can explore the world together and lend our expertise to our governments," I suggest. "Who knows, maybe we'll be raising kids by then."

A grin spreads across his face. "I think I'd like that. Raising children with you. Although do you really want to wait that long?"

I shrug. "Right now, give me time to settle in to

living in a dragon commune. I want to connect with all your people, reconnect with my friends. Maybe see what we can do to encourage more interaction between species. When things are flowing, we can talk about children." I squint thoughtfully. "Did you end up looking into whether I could contribute energy to our egg?" My heart warms just saying it. Our egg. Brandt and I will have an egg together, and then a tiny baby dragon.

Who will grow up to be big enough to carry me.

He nods. "Yes, I consulted the living archive. You can't contribute energy material, but you can contribute energy. It would require you to shift and spend time with my scales and for me to create a conversion spell."

Whoa, that sounds weird. "When you say 'spend time with,' what does that mean? Just be in the room? Or cuddle up to them?"

"Cuddle up to the nest," he confirms. "Or at least be nice and close for a certain time each day. Your energy would transfer via the spell to accumulate with the scale energy."

"That sounds easy enough for me to do." The scales and I could watch daytime TV together. It could be our thing, our bonding time.

"I'll look into it some more," he assures me. "Find out all the details. When we're ready, we'll know everything there is to know." He smiles. "You'd make such beautiful babies."

I lean against him and stare at the lovely late fall landscape, soaking in his warmth and planning our future. Sophie needs some distractions to keep her from driving Kethe nuts with her experiments. Maybe she could get involved in teaching the young ones about Earth—put those experiments to good use. Fabian needs to get out more in a nonsexual sense—he's shockingly naïve about real life. If I get Dustin to go along, maybe he can meet someone to take his attention off his professor. And Steffen… well, that's going to be an epic undertaking. But I get to do it all in this amazing place, surrounded by people who love me.

Percy

FIVE YEARS LATER

"…THINK she's really going to marry him," I tell the egg. It's snug in its nest beside me on the couch in the casual living room on the second floor. Dragon eggs are hard as rocks to begin with but become more delicate as the dragon develops. Once the egg got to the point of changing color from stone gray to a pretty robin's egg blue, signaling that the shell was delicate enough to break, Brandt and I decided it would be safest if the egg wasn't carried up and down stairs. This room was already being used to house his hoard—which, aside from the expected gems and riches, now carefully stored away, is also made up of rare spells and books—so we added a comfy couch, a desk, and TV, converting it into a place he and I could work and people could hang out with the egg and watch TV or read. I usually get quite a lot of company throughout the day—everyone's very excited about a new hatchling.

Today, Brandt's in the city, racing to get through as

much work as possible. The energy vibe from the egg changed last night, which means it could hatch anytime, and he wants to take some time off from the office and get to know our dragonet—and more importantly, help me get used to being the parent of a dragonet. I've never been around one so young before—there's only been two hatchings since the dragons migrated to Earth, and none of them were close by. I've met those babies, cuddled them, even, but not spent any real time with them. So this is going to be a learning experience.

I can't wait.

The last few years have been the best time of my life. I felt needed and wanted and appreciated again, in my element, and the best part was having Brandt at my side. I loved being lucifer, but I was so lonely sometimes. I had Lily, but we both knew that was going nowhere, that we were just friends keeping each other company. Brandt, on the other hand… he's everything. He knows me right down to my soul, and nothing brings me greater joy than knowing I can turn to him for anything, even a casual hug.

I should say nothing *brought* me greater joy. Because over this past year, since our energy transformed into an egg, my whole life has changed. Who would have thought I could get so much pleasure from a one-sided conversation with an egg about a soap opera?

"Did they show who killed Melanie yet?" a voice asks from the doorway, and Dustin comes to join us on the couch. "Hey, egg." He pats it gently, and it pulses affectionately. Brandt and everyone assure me that the dragonet isn't yet able to tell the difference between all the people loving on them, but it does have some awareness—the ability to hear muffled sounds and feel pressure on the eggshell.

"I don't think she's really dead," I counter. "They showed the hand holding the gun, remember, and then the gun firing, but they never showed the bullet hitting her."

On the screen, preparations for the wedding that may or may not actually happen continue. There are a lot of long, dark looks and dramatic pauses from the two bridesmaids who had a threesome with the groom the night before and swore never to tell the bride.

We all know how that's going to go, right?

"So, what, the shooter missed? And then ran away? Have they showed anything more from that storyline yet?" He glances at the clock. "The episode's half over."

I shake my head. "Nothing. They must be building for a dramatic reveal."

We both sigh, then Dustin grins at me.

"You're one worse than the other," Kethe announces from behind us. "Exposing the egg to this drivel." She pretends not to like soaps, but somehow always manages to find a reason to pop in while we're watching.

"The egg loves it," I declare. In truth, I hope the egg doesn't yet understand concepts like murder, infidelity, and blackmail, but there's definitely a special pulse of energy when we settle in to watch TV, so who knows?

She sniffs and squints at the TV. "Have those nasty betrayers broken Raya's heart yet?"

"Not yet," Dustin says. "But I guess it depends on perspective. Didn't they actually break her heart the moment they slept with Chad? And really, did Raya ever have a heart for them to break?"

"Good point," I murmur. Raya's been the character I love to hate for nearly six months now.

Beside me, there's a little shiver of energy from the egg, and I glance over absently.

Then do a double take.

Squeeze my eyes shut and look again.

And make a high-pitched sound that might be a squeal.

Dustin leaps to his feet, looking around wildly. "What?"

I point to the egg and the tiny crack at the top.

"Oh, wow," Dustin says, falling to his knees in front of it and staring. "Oh, wow!"

"I'll get Sophie and call Brandt," Kethe says. "Can I leave you two, or are you going to freak out?"

I shake my head, eyes glued to my soon-to-be baby.

"Percy!" Kethe snaps, and I jerk myself back to reality.

"I'm fine," I assure her, dragging my gaze away to meet hers. "Call Brandt. Tell him to hurry, please." I'm well aware that this could take hours, but I want him here during the hatching, with me and our baby, and I know he wants to be here. "I remember what to do."

Kethe gives me a long, measuring stare but must be satisfied by what she sees, because she heads out the door to find Sophie, digging in her pocket for her cell phone. Dustin and I stay where we are, transfixed by the egg… which is doing nothing. After a few minutes of staring in silence, my step-grandson sighs and says, "We need to pace ourselves."

"We're not doing anything," I point out, but I know what he means. Nothing's going to happen for a long time, and us being all excited is going to make the egg nervous. "Let's finish watching the show."

We settle back on the couch, and I want to rest my hand on the egg as I have so many times before, but it's too fragile right now. Breaking it open before it's ready could traumatize my dragonet, and I'm not letting that happen. Instead, I sit as close to the nest as I can and let it feel my presence. The magic, which has been more and more infrequent a visitor over the years, suddenly rushes around us in an excited flurry.

In my pocket, my phone rings. I dig it out and answer.

"Hi, David." It doesn't surprise me that he somehow knows.

"Brandt's on his way," he assures me. "Are you doing okay? How's the egg?"

"Yes, and good. It's just a tiny crack still. How did you know?"

"Brandt and the king were in a meeting with me and Sam. He ran out of here so fast, I'm surprised he stopped to open the door. Listen, I'm going to hold everyone off for as long as I can, but if you could ask someone to keep us updated, that would help."

"No problem," I assure him as Fabian skids into the room, eyes wide and cheeks flushed. "Fabian is going to be our liaison. He'll update you every hour; sooner if something happens."

"I am?" Fabian asks, and Dustin nods at him.

"Thanks, Percy. I can't wait for you to be a dad," David says, and my breath catches.

"Yeah," I manage. "See you soon." We end the call, and I blink back tears and suck in oxygen. "I'm going to be a dad," I tell Fabian and Dustin.

"Are you only just realizing this? Because it's too late to change your mind," Fabian says worriedly, but Dustin laughs.

"You need to keep David up to date," I tell Fabian, and he nods.

"I can do that. I'll call him now."

"Maybe wait an hour," I suggest, "since I was just speaking to him."

I hear Sophie coming before I see her, and she bursts in with a wide grin. "How exciting!" Her professional gaze skims over the egg, and she nods once in approval. "Let's all sit down and finish watching your show."

SEVEN HOURS LATER, I'm curled up on Brandt's lap beside our egg. The crack has extended almost the entire length of the shell and been joined by several others, spiderwebbing their way across the delicate surface. It's almost time, the egg pulsing regularly now with the energy needed for our dragonet to break out.

The room is quiet. We've had people in and out all afternoon and evening, surrounding our precious baby with love and family, but now that hatching is so close, Sophie cleared them all out. The dragonet needs calm now, not chaos. It's just me and Brandt, with Sophie across the room by the window in case we need her.

Brandt presses his lips to my neck. "I love you. I love you and our baby, and I'm so glad we're here."

I grab his hand, lacing our fingers together. "Love you too," I whisper, turning my head to kiss his cheek, and there's another strong vibration from the egg.

"C'mon, baby," Brandt croons, and he starts to sing

softly. He's been singing to our egg every night since it first transformed, the same elvish lullaby that's been around so long, it never evolved into the modern version of their language. It's in the original, mostly forgotten dialect of their ancestors, and I've never heard anything so beautiful as my lover singing to our child.

Our baby must agree, because with one final pulse of energy, the egg cracks open, shards of shell scattering into the nest, and a tiny, perfect dragonet blinks up at us.

The wave of love that overtakes me is so strong, I can't breathe, but then my daughter chirps, and I suck in a breath and reach for her. She fits in my two hands, palest blue, almost white, from the tip of her nose to the very end of her adorable tail. I cradle her against my chest, and Brandt wraps his arms around both of us.

"What's her name?" Sophie asks quietly, and I glance up to see her standing only a few feet away, smiling at us, misty-eyed.

"Cecylia," Brandt says, and she stirs in my arms.

"I'll go tell everyone she's here," Sophie says. "Call if you need anything." And she leaves us.

"Thank you," Brandt murmurs. "For this. For everything. For not becoming a banker and marrying a stockbroker called Nigel."

I snort and turn my head to meet his lips with mine. Cecylia makes a mewing sound and reaches up to lick our faces, and we break apart, laughing.

"No tongue kisses for you," Brandt says mock sternly, taking her from me. "Not until you're much bigger." I climb out of his lap and go across to the side table where Kethe left a tray of mush—oatmeal and overcooked vegetables—while he croons to her about all the exciting things she has ahead of her. Outside, I hear shouts and cheers as our friends and family celebrate the miracle of a new dragonet, and I know the news will spread fast through our community. We're going to have a lot of visitors over the next few days, lots of gifts and well-wishing messages.

But for now, all that's important is right here in this room as Brandt and I feed our daughter her first meal.

Thanks so much for reading *Dragon Ever After*! If you'd like to read about Percy's *actual* naked dragon ride, you can grab the bonus scene by subscribing to my newsletter: bit.ly/LouisaMBonus

Next, it's Dustin's turn to find true love in *The Professor's Dragon.*

If you'd like to read about all the things that happened to bring Brandt and the dragons to Earth, check out my Hidden Species series, starting with *Demons Do It Better.* You'll get to see all Percy's friends fall in love.

We talk spoilers in my Facebook Reader Group: RoMMance With Becca & Louisa.

And for early access to chapters of my upcoming books, artwork, and other bonus material, check out my Patreon here: patreon.com/louisamasters

ALSO BY LOUISA MASTERS

Saddles & Suits

Alistair's Extraordinaries

Grave Situation

Elemental Men: The Complete Series

Style Me

Rebrand

Couture

Elf Magic

Wooing the Wiccan

Enticing the Elf

The Collective

Higher Demon

Demon Hunter

Demons-In-Law

Asher

Micah

Zachary

Franklin U

Mr. Romance

The Holigay Hookup *related novella

Batting Style

Ghostly Guardians

Spirited Situation

Vortex Conundrum

Conduit Crisis

Gateway Catastrophe

Here Be Dragons

Dragon Ever After

The Professor's Dragon

The Dragon Experiment

Conspiracy of Dragons

Hidden Species

Demons Do It Better

One Bite With A Vampire

Hijinks With A Hellhound

Sorcerers Always Satisfy

Hidden Species Box Set

Met His Match

<u>Charming Him</u>

<u>Offside Rules</u>

<u>A Christmas Chance (novella)</u>

<u>Between the Covers (M/F)</u>

Joy Universe

I've Got This

<u>Follow My Lead</u>

<u>In Your Hands</u>

ABOUT THE AUTHOR

Louisa Masters started reading romance much earlier than her mother thought she should. As an adult, she feeds her addiction in every spare second. She spent years trying to build a "sensible" career, working in bookstores, recruitment, resource management, administration, and as a travel agent before finally conceding defeat and devoting herself to the world of romance novels.

Louisa has a long list of places first discovered in books that she wants to visit, and every so often she overcomes her loathing of jet lag and takes a trip that charges her imagination. She lives in Melbourne, Australia, where she whines about the weather for most of the year while secretly admitting she'll probably never move.

http://www.louisamasters.com